# One Last Kiss

Books by Mary Wilbon

NAUGHTY LITTLE SECRETS
ONE LAST KISS

Published by Kensington Publishing Corporation

# One Last Kiss

## MARY WILBON

KENSINGTON BOOKS
http://www.kensingtonbooks.com

KENSINGTON BOOKS are published by

Kensington Publishing Corp.
850 Third Avenue
New York, NY 10022

All Kensington titles, imprints, and distributed lines are available at special quantity discounts for bulk purchases for sales promotion, premiums, fund-raising, educational, or institutional use.

Special book excerpts or customized printings can also be created to fit specific needs. For details, write or phone the office of the Kensington Special Sales Manager: Attn. Special Sales Department. Kensington Publishing Corp., 850 Third Avenue, New York, NY 10022. Phone: 1-800-221-2647.

Kensington and the K logo Reg. U.S. Pat. & TM Off.

ISBN-13: 978-0-7582-1599-4
ISBN-10: 0-7582-1599-1

First Kensington Trade Paperback Printing: March 2009
10  9  8  7  6  5  4  3  2  1

Printed in the United States of America

*For G,*
*I can still hear your song*

# Acknowledgments

Thanks to my editor at Kensington Books, John Scogna-miglio, for giving me another opportunity. He makes me want to do better and reach higher.

Thanks to all the other folks I leaned on to get this book done:

Joseph Petrecca, Raymond Martoccia, and Dr. Jonathan Coleman for answering my questions.

Samuel Billings, Catherine F. Sutherland, Maria Pires, Nancy Vazquez, and Paula Ruffin—my work family.

John Warner for giving me a new enthusiasm for my old job.

Kate Daly, Lisa Alford, and all the STOP KISS-ers for calling me out to play.

Thanks to Deliah Clarke for showing me Paradise.

Thanks to Ethel DiMicele. Some things were meant to last.

A very special thanks to my forever friends Maureen and Joanne and their families. I met Mo and Jo in high school, and there hasn't been a day since that I couldn't depend on them to share their time or their hearts when I've needed them.

Cynthia S. Ross and Rob Pape were so kind for giving their talents and time, and they took turns holding my hand whenever I stopped writing. Thank you.

Thanks to Doug Mendini for slapping my hand when I stopped writing and for pushing me and inspiring me to start writing again.

# Prologue

The men in the room looked at each other, wondering how they were going to handle the problem that loomed before them. Collectively, these men had hundreds of secrets, but this evening they were concentrating on only one.

It was a delicate matter that only men of culture and importance could discuss and resolve tactfully. Earlier they had ordered and enjoyed their thick steaks, prepared blood-rare and sipped three rounds of Glenfiddich thirty-year-old scotch while discussing business deals, politics, and the next promising stocks that were about to explode big-time in the market.

The small talk had died down, and they were now smoking cigars and blowing smoke rings at each other. The gentlemen glanced around at one another nervously. The unpleasant business they had to address left many of them sitting in silence.

But they all agreed on one thing: They had to get their hands on the journal. It was the only thing that linked them together outside of this private club. Inside these walls, they knew the prevailing rule: survival at all costs.

The whore had to be dealt with, and her journal had to be destroyed. It all sounded so sensible and reasonable. They all enjoyed the whore, but who knew she had kept the journal? It was a worrisome development. They thought their power and position had made them untouchable in such matters. Those things had always worked in the past.

The senator, the most powerful of them, tapped on his glass of port until he had their attention. He was a fleshy red-faced man, the eldest in the group, with a thick shock of white hair and caterpillar-sized eyebrows. He had the look of a man who had been handsome once, long ago, but whose looks were now fading fast.

"Gentlemen, do we all agree that we have a problem?" he asked.

Rumblings of agreement rippled through the room.

The senator knew they were all listening now, so he continued. "Of course. We've all . . . shall we say . . . taken our pleasure with her. But now the whore has become a threat to all of us, and she must be eliminated. Swiftly."

More affirmative chatter.

"This can't come back to bite any of us. Whatever it takes, this whole thing gets buried."

And there it was. They were talking about murder. They all knew it, even while they were still skirting around the edges of the subject.

Only one man voiced an objection. All eyes turned to where he sat at the end of the table.

He rose to address them. He was the youngest man in the room, but he had earned their respect.

"Why are you doing this?" he asked. "What gives you the right?"

The senator shot the young man a disappointed look.

"We have no choice," someone answered.

"You're all afraid of some journal or diary she may be keeping. You don't know for sure that she is," he argued.

"She has a record of all our names and phone numbers. That's dangerous," said the senator.

"Isn't it enough that she's going away?" the young man asked.

"No, it is not enough. There are no guarantees that she won't someday start blackmailing us," came another response.

"If she wanted to blackmail us, she could have done that long ago. She's never done a thing to hurt or embarrass any of us. And she has had ample opportunity," he reminded them.

The responses stopped. Maybe there was a chance they wouldn't have to go through with their plan. The senator knew he had to pull them back from their ambivalence, tap into their fear.

"She tried to quit before," the senator prompted them. "She changed her mind. She may change her mind again in the future," he suggested.

The rumbling started up again.

"Listen to me," said the young opponent. "All she wants to do is get as far away as possible from the life she has led up until now. We trusted her to keep our secrets in the past. She has never betrayed any of us, has she?"

Looks were exchanged around the room. He was right; they had to agree. The whore was selected partially for her well-known discretion.

"I think she can be trusted to keep quiet about us."

"And what if she's not successful in her new life?" the senator asked.

Now they all began talking at once, sounding like an angry mob.

"She may decide it would be very profitable to write her memoirs."

"Or sit down and have a chat with Oprah."

"We have to act now, or these matters could come to light at a most inopportune time."

"We could all be ruined and lose everything."

"She's a cancer that must be cut out."

It was useless. They were not listening to him. The young man felt like a ghost from another time. He looked at the senator. He was not talking now but sat silently sipping his port, seeming pleased with himself that the rest had aligned with him.

The man walked over and grabbed the senator's arm before he could raise the port to his lips again.

"This is murder you're talking about. You're crossing a line you will never be able to step back from."

"We'll risk it. The stakes are too high." The senator broke free of the man's grip on his arm and took a long sip of his port.

The man scanned the faces of the other men in the room and knew they had decided against him. The girl had become a threat swirling around their cherished upper-class lives. Nothing he could say was going to change their minds.

"I don't want any part of this," he said. "If anything happens to her, if she twists her ankle, if she breaks a nail, I promise I'll come after you. I'll find you, and I'll do whatever I can to see you get the justice you deserve."

Then he walked out.

A few attempted to stop him, but it was useless. He forced his way past them and was gone.

"Let him go," the senator said casually. "He'll come around. He has as much to lose as the rest of us." The senator stood up now to address them further. "I'll take care of it. I know someone the whore trusts. He'll see that the problem is fixed—disposed of properly." He sipped his port.

Then the questions started.

"Are you sure he can be trusted?"

"Yes, this man is perfect," he assured them.

"Perfect how?"

"When it is done, he will be the perfect scapegoat. We'll use him, then throw him away. He won't be missed." Another silence. "Any other questions, gentlemen?" No one spoke.

"I will make sure the whore goes away permanently. It's extreme, but it's the only move we have. Put your minds at ease. There will be one less of these miserable bitches to prey on our weaknesses."

The mood in the room became jovial again. There was a tasteful round of restrained applause and the relighting of cigars.

"We will never speak of it again, and this won't cost you a thing," he said.

"We will be in your debt forever," someone said casually.

"Yes, you will, won't you . . . forever. I'll let you know when and if I intend to collect on that debt."

He raised his glass and toasted them.

"Good night, gentlemen."

Every eye was on him as he left.

Then there was a crashing silence. The powerful men in the room let it sink in for a moment just what that debt might cost them. No one said a word. No one even blinked.

## This Is Action News 10 in New Jersey . . . All of New Jersey All of the Time

"Good morning. I'm Michelle Tevotino. Republican Pete Moreno now has a seven percent advantage in New Jersey's U.S. Senate campaign. The latest election poll in the Garden State shows Moreno leading Democrat challenger Clinton Kendall forty-three percent to thirty-six percent. Seven percent of voters say that they will vote for some other candidate, an independent, or write-in, and fourteen percent remain undecided in this Democratic-leaning state. A month ago, Moreno held a two percent advantage. Moreno has solidified support among Republicans since the last poll, while Kendall has lost ground among Democrats. From an ideological perspective, Family Values Moreno has improved his standing with conservative voters in the state.

"And for the second time, New Jersey voters will decide on a bond for special development improvements. Supporters of the bond claim that the monies would be used to promote smart growth and improve quality of life. The goal is to rebuild cities with an emphasis on residential construction and therefore increase the tax base. The first three target areas would be Newark, Trenton, and Camden. Opponents of the bond proposals claim that there is no way to ensure the money would be used appropriately and that approving the bond would lead to an increase in taxes. The bond failed to pass in the last election when seventy-seven percent of the voters said nay.

"In other news, a twenty-six-year-old unidentified man from Jackson, New Jersey, choked to death on a sequined pastie while getting a lap dance at a local strip club last night. The exotic dancer, identified only as 'Ginger,' had this to say to our Action 10 in New Jersey News crew: 'He was sucking on my . . . um . . . titties . . . oops (giggle snort), I mean, bosoms when he orally removed the three-inch plastic pastie. He started chewing it while he was laughing. It was all in good fun. I didn't think he was going to actually try to swallow it, ya know what I mean? Those things aren't edible. He was really drunk. I'm a little hungover myself, ya know what I mean?'" (giggle snort)

# 1

Slick and Laura went over the plan one more time. Laura was tired and apprehensive, and she fumbled her part.

"Damn it," she said. "Just call me butterfingers."

Laura didn't curse often, but when she did, Slick knew she had reached her limit.

Laura was still skeptical about this new assignment. She stood up and walked around the room, deep in thought. She stopped at the window and looked out.

Garbo, who was practicing with them, grabbed hold of Laura's pant leg and wouldn't let go. Laura laughed in spite of herself. She stroked the dog's head. Garbo immediately let go of her pant leg, wiggled her hind quarters, and rolled over on her back to get more.

Laura shook her head in exasperation

"What's wrong?" Slick asked.

"Garbo is better at this than I am. I'm not sure I'm ready."

"Of course you are."

"Did you see me drop the package?"

"So you made a mistake."

"I dropped it before, too," Laura reminded her.

"That's why we practice," Slick said encouragingly.

Laura looked doubtful. "I can't afford to make a mistake. You're depending on me."

"We'll do it again. You'll get it right next time."

Laura, irritated with herself, kicked the package she had been practicing with. "Damn it! I haven't gotten it right yet! Why do you keep saying I can do this?"

Slick came up behind her and encircled Laura in her arms. Laura's head was a nice fit beneath her chin.

"Because you can, that's why. You know the drill."

Laura relaxed and pulled Slick's arms tighter around her.

"I know it, but I'm worried I'll screw it up," she said softly. "This is a big deal with big consequences."

"You're just a little nervous."

"Nervous! I'm scared stiff. I've got goose bumps the size of tomatoes."

"You can do this, Laura."

Laura sighed and tilted her head to look at Slick. "Why can't you have a regular nine-to-five job?"

Slick laughed and pulled her closer. "Why did you leave your regular nine-to-five job to join me in this?" she asked.

Slick nuzzled and kissed her head, savoring the smell of the shampoo on Laura's long blond hair, which tickled Slick's nose.

Laura smiled. She sure hadn't started out doing this line of work.

She looked out the window of the home her father had built. A sixty-two-room mansion on 30,000 acres in the sprawling Ramapo Mountains in New Jersey.

Laura's father, Owen Charles, had left her independently wealthy. He had made a fortune in the 1950s in New Jersey's clamming industry. Laura was his only child, and even though

Owen could be a ruthless businessman and a philandering husband, he had worshipped Laura.

She grew up in this house, surrounded by all the things money could buy, and she inherited everything. She knew at an early age that she was gay, so she never married, never had children. She ran the business well and made some significant improvements. No one could accuse her of simply living on her father's famous name.

She had been comfortable running the business she inherited and living the life of a wealthy socialite when she met and fell in love with Slick, a black female cop from Newark. The fact that they met, fell in love, and stayed there was a miracle.

Slick moved in, and after years of spirited and often loud debate, Laura finally convinced her to quit the police force and work at the clam company. This happened when a fellow officer took a bullet in the shoulder from a crack-crazed kid. That was the last straw for Laura. Slick eventually agreed, but she never lost her desire for police work.

A few years earlier, when Laura's longtime butler, Judson, asked her for help in a murder case that involved his niece, Slick jumped at the chance to get back into detective work, and Laura joined her. They solved the case, and Laura never went back to work at the clam company.

"Okay," Laura admitted, "I like working cases. I've enjoyed every minute of it until now. This one is different. This guy is dangerous. Very dangerous."

"Dangerous, yes, but not unpredictable. He's developed a pattern. He's acted in a very specific and methodical way. And that is how we're going to catch him."

"What if he suspects something? He won't show if he thinks it's a trap."

"Then we can always catch him another time. He's good at what he does, Laura. He won't quit. This won't be the end for him if we don't stop him now."

Laura was thoughtful. "Is it wrong of me to wish he doesn't show up?"

Slick laughed. "No, but I'd like to help get him. Wouldn't you?"

"I suppose, but . . ."

"Look, there'll be protection everywhere on the street, and we'll be in constant communication with them."

"Accidents still happen. If anything happened to you . . ."

"I'll be fine," Slick assured her.

"You better. We're going on vacation when this thing is over. We've earned it."

"You know, I'm not the only one taking a risk here, Laura. What you're doing in this operation is not without some danger."

"Not like you."

"We've run through every security threat possible. You know how people always say, 'It'll be fine. Everything's going to be okay'? Well, this really is going to be okay."

Slick wondered if her words sounded as hollow to Laura as they did to her. She believed what she was saying, but it did sound lame.

Laura looked at her and nodded. Without conviction, Slick thought.

"For you it's just another day on the job. I'm a babe in the woods on this," Laura said.

"You are a babe for sure, but you're getting good at this detective stuff. Look at how far you've come since our first case. You have great instincts, and I need you."

Laura leaned back against her. "Say it again and make me believe it."

Slick turned her around and looked deeply in her eyes.

"I do need you. I work better with a partner. I was a good cop, but having Sam with me made me a better one. We were a team. Now you and I are the team."

Laura seemed to brighten a little.

"Besides, Laura, I know you. You started this, and I know you want to see how it ends. Am I right?"

"Yeah, I guess so."

"We're going to laugh about this when it's over."

"What if it turns out to be a disaster?"

Slick shrugged. "Then it was all your idea," she said. "That's the other good thing about having a partner—you can blame someone else."

Laura punched her playfully.

"You know it's a good plan. It will work."

"Then we might as well see it through."

"That's my girl," Slick said proudly.

They wouldn't have to talk about it again.

Laura clapped her hands. Garbo sat at attention. Slick resumed practice mode.

"Okay, suit up, you two," Laura said with renewed vigor. "We're going in."

# 2

Another Friday night was fast approaching on Halsey Street in Newark. The children of the night were busily preparing for the weekend sex trade. Strip club and XXX movie theater owners swept the floors and took cursory swipes at the mixture of dried bodily goop on the seats.

The massage parlors and the rent-by-the-hour motels doubled their staffs to cover the next forty-eight hours. The sex novelty store owners restocked their shelves with dildos, butt plugs, bondage supplies, edible undies, and the latest desensitizing lotions for the premature ejaculate/sore anus crowd.

As darkness fell, the prostitutes began to walk "the stroll" in timed strides. The air was filled with the rising sounds of whistles, catcalls, car horns, and giggles.

Variety is the spice of life, and the great variety of ages, races, body shapes, and specialty acts available on Halsey Street was more than enough to scratch any fantasy itch. Straight, gay, bi, or trans, there was ample outlet for anyone's inner freak.

Sex was for sale every day of the week on Halsey Street,

but the weekends brought more hustle and bustle, emphasis on the hustle.

Businessmen on business trips wanting to fast-forward to the juicy bits cruised the streets looking for the no-strings-attached screw before returning home. Car doors would open and prices were negotiated.

Cut-to-the-quick suck or fuck.

College boys, classes done for the week, looking now to party, dared each other to do a prostitute at least once. It was so entertaining to the workers. Young men, especially the big jocks, nervously approached the whores; then most walked away quickly. A few stayed. It all depended on the come-on. Some of the older, more experienced, pros had all the amorous charm of used-car salesmen. The younger ones had perfected an appealing come-hither look—lips pursed, eyelashes batting, topped off with a shy innocent blush, smile, and look-away act.

No matter what the approach, none of these sex providers felt exploited. Most were drug and disease free and insisted on double methods of protection. They looked at prostitution as a short stop on their way to greater things. They felt that purchased whoopee was just another service for sale. Money paid for services provided. No more exploitive than any money paid to your mechanic or your dentist.

The police patrolling Halsey Street kept a low profile. They made some token arrests of the prostitutes from time to time but usually stepped in only when big-time drug dealers tried to come in and sell heavy drugs or when pimps tried to harass the streetwalkers. It worked that way for years. The area wasn't residential, so very few locals complained about it. The shop owners who weren't involved in the sale of sex-related merchandise were closed and gone for the day before the action really got going.

The police often started here when looking for bigger busts, because this was a portal to whatever was happening on the streets. No matter what the criminal activity, someone on Halsey Street had information about it. And for the most part, the streetwalkers cooperated; they were the eyes and ears for the cops, because they knew the police let them sell their more fun parts.

So, it was the start of just another Friday night on Halsey Street, swelling up with a thousand different ways to separate sex from love.

Streetwalking regulars Lady Dijonnaise and Sheleeta Buffet ambled through the crowds, taking in the Friday night sights and sounds. The twin six-foot-seven, 350-pound black transvestites, who had begun life as Cletis and Cleotis Stubbs, respectively, were well known. According to urban legend, they once had been pro wrestlers turned celebrity bodyguards and now, cross-dressing hookers.

Lady and Sheleeta stopped and exchanged friendly banter with the sex workers as they made their way down the street. There was an easygoing feeling of camaraderie among the hookers. They understood one another, and they looked out for one another. Tonight, all the talk was about the bond issue that was soon to be voted on. If it passed, many of the workers were afraid that the city would begin to seriously go after them, clear them off the street to make way for the shiny new office towers, shopping malls, and residential communities. It had already happened in other sections of Newark. The city was trying to bounce back from years of depression. As the city rebuilt, the sex workers lost territory. Halsey Street was one of the few remaining areas where no one really bothered them.

Lady and Sheleeta tried to assure the hookers that the bond issue would never pass.

"This is going to be another good night on the stroll." Lady Dijonnaise laughed excitedly as she looked at the waves of horny humanity flowing by.

"The sweet smell of cock is in the air!" She threw her head back and inhaled deeply, savoring the smell.

"No, honey, I just burped," Sheleeta replied, and fanned at the air in front of her face, trying to make the burp disappear. "You probably just smellin' my last trick's dick area. I can still taste it. Oh, he had a lovely man region. Just lovely. Succulent! Wonderfully maintained! Fragrant like the first day of spring. His balls were elegantly trimmed and coiffed, cut to highlight a super-sized King Kong unit. But, sadly, his big monkey's spunky was a little funky."

Sheleeta reached into her purse and pulled out a tin of Altoids. She was about to pop one into her mouth when her attention was drawn to a beautiful Japanese woman approaching. Sheleeta became rigid with emotion. The woman who stopped Sheleeta in her tracks was the former Mr. Haiku Ono, a recently transgendered hooker known as Spicy Tuna.

Spicy saw Sheleeta and quickly crossed the street to get away.

"You better step off before I throw some wasabi whoop-ass on you!" Sheleeta shouted as Spicy retreated. Seconds later, Sheleeta was trembling, almost in tears.

Lady went to Sheleeta and tried to give comfort. "Now, girl, don't be reliving your personal tragedy out here on the street. Walk on. Be strong."

"Tell that to my heart! My wounds haven't healed! I'm still in pain," Sheleeta blurted out. "That bitch poisoned my cat! Then she took the carcass and threw it on my porch. Oh, the ugliness! The carnage! I can still hear the screams."

"You were the one screaming, Sheleeta," Lady reminded her. "The cat had been dead for hours."

"I'm having a flashback."

Now Sheleeta was brimming with tears.

"You're right, honey. Sure you're right. That girl served you up a big steaming bowl of WRONG. But Spicy was off her lithium at the time. You know she is crazy as hell when she is off that shit," Lady tried to reason.

Sheleeta nodded in understanding and tried bravely to suck up her tears of grief.

"But Peesonthechaise was a wonderful cat, wasn't he?" Her words were choked and halting. Her lower lip began to quiver. Soon, Sheleeta lost the battle and collapsed into a sobbing, wailing wreck. Fortunately, there was enough Kleenex in her purse for crisis tear-dabbing and nose-blowing.

Lady Dijonnaise wrapped her massive arms around the massive Sheleeta Buffet in a big bear hug. They each felt the other's beard stubble.

"I mourn that cat every day, too, Sheleeta."

Lady hated herself for lying to her brother/sister. There had been times when Lady wanted to stuff Peesonthechaise down the garbage disposal, but she couldn't figure out a way to make the gruesome death look accidental. She was glad the little bastard was dead, and she was secretly grateful to Spicy Tuna for taking him out.

Lady looked up and down the street for something to take Sheleeta's mind off her dead cat. If Sheleeta didn't stop crying soon, she'd start to hiccup uncontrollably. When that happened, she looked like a big-ass widemouthed frog on steroids.

Lady had to stop the crying now. Her eyes scanned Halsey

Street. Then, miraculously, she saw what she was looking for and smiled broadly.

"Who wants to split a bucket of Original Recipe?" she cooed.

"Oh, the Colonel! I'd love some. I'm already having a delish-o-gasm!"

Sheleeta broke free of Lady's arms and bounded across the street toward the KFC, her Manolo Blahniks straining under the load. She looked like a small army tank racing toward a target.

Lady and Sheleeta ordered, then took their food to a table with a window view of Halsey Street. It was dark now, and there was an electricity sparking the night that was both edgy and entertaining, like an open-air carnival.

Lady was dividing up the food and napkins when, again, Sheleeta stopped cold.

"Not Spicy Tuna again. Let it go, Sheleeta." Lady had had enough of the Peesonthechaise lament for tonight, and she was hungry.

"No! No! Look who's back." Sheleeta was excitedly pointing across the street.

Lady looked out the big window and saw a beautiful black woman with long legs, clearly defined calves, and firm thighs coming up the street. She had the face of an angel and flawless dark skin, and although she was obviously mature, she still had the ripe body of a teenager—eager, full, and lush. Her breasts stretched the top she was wearing to its fiber limit. She was the stuff wet fantasies were made of. The sexual energy she exuded spilled over beyond gender boundaries. She was clearly distinguishable, even through the manic blur of people now overtaking Halsey Street.

Lady turned back to Sheleeta. "You're right. It is her. It's Paradise."

Paradise had set herself apart long ago from the other prostitutes on Halsey Street. It wasn't about the money for her. She really enjoyed the sex. She hadn't run to the streets because her momma didn't understand her or because her daddy didn't love her enough.

She wanted the opportunity to explore her sexuality. She loved the feel of sex, the soreness of it, the sweet delightful invasion of the body that lasts for days. Paradise brought her love of sex to all her clientele. She had politicians, doctors, lawyers, and a few celebrities begging for her.

Sheleeta watched Paradise in awe.

"I heard that girl is a one-woman whore extravaganza," she said respectfully.

"Oh yes, honey. Paradise is an *artiste* in the art of whore. People pay some crazy cash to get with her," Lady confirmed. Then she looked around the KFC to make sure no one was listening. She leaned in confidentially close to Sheleeta and asked in a hushed reverential tone, "Did you ever hear the story about the Smilin' Man?"

"The Smilin' Man? No!"

"Well, the word is that Paradise's honey pot tastes so good, that first this john went down on her and it was so sweet he didn't want to go any further. He thought that after such good-tasting pussy, intercourse would be a letdown. So Paradise dared him to fuck her but warned him it would be more than he could stand. So now, of course, the john HAD to do her, so he stuck his dick in her, and her squeeze box was so tight, it felt like a Vulcan death grip. When it was over, the john died on top of her. Very happy. Even the undertaker couldn't get the blissful smile off that man's face."

"Shut up!"

"I am serious, honey. That poor undertaker lost his business because of it."

"No!"

"Hell, yes! The Smilin' Man's wife sued his ass for pain and suffering and won; then she closed that motherfucker down."

"What!"

"The funeral was real embarrassing for her. She was humiliated. Just imagine. Their family and friends coming to pay their respects at the funeral parlor. People they both knew and socialized with. And there was her husband, lying all up in the coffin, smiling in death, looking happier than he had ever been in his whole entire life."

"No shit!" Sheleeta said in wonder.

"I shit you not, little sisterman!"

Lady and Sheleeta watched Paradise as she approached the corner. Then she turned and began talking with someone who was standing in shadows. Lady and Sheleeta tried to see who it was but couldn't.

"Who's that she's talking to? Is it that cop that used to hang around her?" Sheleeta asked, struggling to see what was going on.

"I don't know, Sheleeta. It could be Hugh Grant or Eddie Murphy for all I know. I can't tell from here. But it better not be that no-good Jimmy Swaggart again. The sex stuff he wanted from some of the workers was so freaky, it would scare the heebie-jeebies out of Charles Fuckin' Manson."

Lady watched closely. She was concerned. She was very protective of the sex providers.

Lady and Sheleeta watched as Paradise started to walk

away from whoever she was talking to but was pulled into the shadows, completely out of their sight.

Seconds later, Paradise tried to walk away again, and again she was pulled back, this time more forcefully.

"I don't like the looks of this," Lady said, and headed out the door. Sheleeta was right behind her.

By the time they were able to elbow and shove their way through the moving throng, as only large determined men in wigs and high heels can do, and reach the spot where Paradise had been standing, she was gone, almost as if she'd never been there.

Lady and Sheleeta looked everywhere on the crowded street. They frantically questioned everyone in the area. Paradise had been noticed, of course, but no one had seen her leave. Lady and Sheleeta split up and stood at opposite ends of the street, searching the crowd for hours. But there was no sign of Paradise anywhere.

She had simply vanished into the Friday night din of Halsey Street.

# 3

As always, the night beckoned to Hamilton Baker. He loved his late-night jogs. He jogged every night, barring inclement weather, year-round. He wasn't ready for summer to end, but despite his wishes, the days were growing shorter.

The mix of streetlight spilling onto the ground and the moon above had a tranquilizing effect on him. He savored the quiet time. He looked up at the silver sickle of moon against a dark sky that seemed to envelop him.

This Friday had been particularly stressful. He had to prepare for his closing argument before a jury. He had rehearsed it in his head, over and over. Being a workaholic, he had worked obsessively for more than a year in preparation. He arrived at the office at 7:00 A.M., and he worked weekends. The hard work paid off, because now Hamilton was a rising star in the DA's office.

He knew exactly what to expect on Monday morning. The courtroom would be in total silence, waiting for him to begin. He would push his chair away dramatically from the prosecution table, slowly approach the jury box, and give his stunning summation.

The mixed-race jury of nine men and three women would adjourn to the jury room, then deliver a guilty verdict for the murdering bitch. Kimberly Shaw murdered her husband, New Jersey real estate tycoon Michael Shaw, by shattering his skull with a heavy bronze sculpture. There was no evidence of a break-in, and Mr. Shaw had not been entertaining or expecting a visitor that evening.

Hamilton was certain he had convinced them of the woman's guilt. And, more important, the jury liked Hamilton. He could feel it. But you never really knew for sure. Juries could be unpredictable.

His office needed to win this case. The homicide rate was on the rise. His bosses at the prosecutor's office let him know that every chance they got, and they had been in his office practically every ten minutes this Friday before his Monday summation to remind him.

In particular, his boss, DA Jeffrey Barnes, was always leaving messages for how Hamilton should behave in front of the cameras and microphones that were always waiting for him outside the courtroom. And that's why Hamilton was stressed out and in need of this quiet time.

He checked his cell phone for messages. He kept his office informed of his every move during a case. There were no messages. No one was looking for him.

He inhaled deeply, feeling the pressure of the workday falling away, and started to relax. Starting slowly, he picked up a comfortable speed, letting the autumn wind blow through his hair, and enjoyed the freedom of the night. He felt completely alive. Orson, his black Lab, trotted at his side. Dry leaves cartwheeled and crackled as they moved.

He headed toward his favorite spot in Mountainside,

Echo Lake Park. Once he entered the park, there was only the sound of his own breathing, his footfalls, the crickets, and the rest of the insect chorus. An owl stirred in the trees and asked his name as he went by.

A deer raised her head, trembling and listening as she picked up the sound of a twig snapping. She turned her head. Usually the park animals didn't trouble themselves to avoid the late joggers, almost as if they sensed the runners meant them no harm. If they were nibbling on some leaves, they'd continue doing so.

Something else was approaching. It was a car, far up the path. It sped past Hamilton, then swerved left, angling down the park's central road, and was swallowed by the shadows.

Hamilton's cell phone started to vibrate. He stumbled off the running trail and checked the readout. He smiled and decided to take the call.

Orson continued to trot ahead, picking up a scent.

"Hello, Sarah," he said. Sarah Donner was his fiancée.

"Am I interrupting?" she asked.

"Not at all. Just out for a run with Orson."

"How do you think it went today?"

"My closing argument is done. I'm happy with it. I'm pretty confident they'll convict."

"I know they will. You're the best prosecutor in that office."

"You're just saying that because you're going to marry me."

"I'm saying that because I'm going to marry the best prosecutor in that office. Don't let Orson keep you out too late. Get some rest."

"Will you have dinner with me tomorrow?"

"Of course. Call me in the morning."

"You know, you could come over tonight and help me relieve some of the stress and tension."

"I'd love to, but I don't want to be a distraction. You do need to sleep."

"I'll sleep better if you're next to me."

"Are you sure?"

"Very."

"Then I'll be at your place in an hour."

"Okay, Sarah. Love you." He ended the call.

There came an outburst of Orson barking. At first Hamilton thought he was barking at another big dog, because Orson was really making a racket. The dog was alternately crouching and running circles around someone in the park.

Orson's behavior looked anything but playful.

Hamilton broke into a run. The last thing he needed right now, at the end of his big case, was to get involved in a nasty dog-bite incident.

He ran faster.

Ahead, Orson continued barking. Now he could see what was upsetting him. A man was lunging with both arms at Orson.

The man looked around and seemed to reach for something in his pocket.

"Hey!" Hamilton called out as he drew closer.

The man straightened up quickly and withdrew his hand from his pocket.

He looked around quickly, nervously.

"Orson, come."

But Orson was in manic mode and barely acknowledged Hamilton. The dog was lowered on his haunches, growling and panting as if readying to launch at the stranger.

Hamilton prepared for trouble.

"He bite you?" he asked.

The man shook his head, trying to keep his head low.

But Hamilton didn't want to take any chances. He was the lead attorney in a high-profile case, and he didn't want any bad press.

Hamilton keyed up the cell phone's menu and engaged the camera function. He started to videotape the scene. The man looked up, startled.

"I just want proof, buddy. I don't want to be sued later."

He saw the man clearly. Tall with dark clothes, a cowboy hat.

The man seemed to panic. "I said I'm all right."

Then he ran away. Hamilton could hear him breathing fast, could feel his determination.

Orson began barking again and started to chase him. For a moment, Hamilton thought the dog might catch him. "Orson, stop."

Orson slowed down and stopped running eventually, and the man disappeared into the night.

Orson ceased barking, and the park returned to silence.

Hamilton checked the phone and the image of the man that was there. He was happy he got the man on tape, proof positive that the dog had not injured him.

What Hamilton didn't see was that the car the man had driven was now partially submerged in Echo Lake.

Hamilton continued with his nightly jog while the lake water gently lapped against the car.

# 4

Before she could scream, his right hand closed over her mouth. He lifted his knee like a punch, deep into her stomach, and then stepped back. She collapsed onto the floor at his feet.

He watched her gasp for breath, writhing like a fish out of water. He looked down at her.

This was the woman they were all so afraid of? It was comical.

She was rolling on the floor bumping into furniture, fighting to breathe. She would scream soon, but she couldn't do that until she got her breath back, and by then . . .

"If you give me what I want, you could still leave here alive."

She emitted small gasping sounds, her eyes wide open as she continued to gasp for air.

"Where is your diary?"

She started to cough. She was getting air now.

He walked to a table and picked up the bag he brought. Pulling out a knife, he held it up for her to see.

This made her panic and added to her breathing diffi-culty. "I don't have the diary," she struggled to say.

He ran his thumb along the knife's sharp blade. "This is just for you, but if you tell me what you did with the diary, you will live." He walked toward her with the knife. "You're so beautiful. I understand the power you have."

He knelt down, ran the knife along her cheek, and stopped at her throat. "Don't move," he whispered chillingly.

She froze.

"Now tell me where it is."

"I told you, I don't have it."

"I'm running out of patience," he said sternly.

"I don't have the diary. I got rid of it, I swear. If I had it, I'd give it to you," she said between coughing fits.

"Then where is it?"

She said nothing.

"WHERE IS IT?"

Again she resisted but started to cry.

"Is this a secret you really want to die for?"

"I put it in the mail."

"To whom?"

"To Laura Charles."

"Laura Charles?"

"Yes. To her foundation."

He looked at her in disbelief and involuntarily withdrew the knife a little.

"Why there?" he asked, truly puzzled.

"I know why," another man said.

Gloria looked at the other man standing in the shadows. She hadn't noticed him until now.

"Help me, please," Gloria begged him.

He avoided her eyes. "I'll take care of it. Let's just get this over with." He had no stomach for this.

The man with the knife looked at him. "Okay, I believe you." He returned his attention to Gloria and ran the knife around her face again.

She recoiled.

"I'm sorry. I can't let you live after all, but you are so beautiful. I won't destroy your face."

She was sobbing now.

"I'll save this for later." He put down the knife and placed his hands on either side of her face. "Don't worry, this will be quick."

"Please help me," she called out to the other man, but he did nothing.

She started to cry. "Please God, no."

"Ssh, shh," he said.

With his hands on either side of her head, he quickly twisted her neck as far as he could.

There was a snap of bones.

Her open eyes seemed to find the one she called out to for help.

And he, the other man in the shadows, full of fear and regret, wondered how he would live with the memory of her murder.

## This Is Action News 10 in New Jersey . . . All of New Jersey All of the Time

"Good morning. I'm Michelle Tevotino. Thanks for joining us. With only a few weeks left until the elections, Action News 10 in New Jersey will host a live debate tonight between senatorial candidates Clinton Kendall and Pete Moreno. This is one of the most closely watched Senate races in the country.

"Liberal Democrat Kendall and conservative Republican Moreno couldn't be further apart on the issues, from the war, stem-cell research, abortion, and same-sex marriage. The latest polls show Kendall with a slight lead over Moreno but still within the margin of error. The president and the war continue to hurt the Republican candidate, but he continues to have strong approval numbers across New Jersey's Democrat-leaning electorate. A Moreno victory would be a major upset in the heavily Democratic state of New Jersey. Tune in tonight to Action News 10 in New Jersey at eight P.M. for what promises to be a very exciting exchange.

"In other news, a Keansburg, New Jersey, man, convicted in the shooting death of his girlfriend's toy poodle, was told he could reduce his jail sentence by dressing like a dog. Daryl Covey was sentenced to thirty days, but Judge Warren Medina said time would be reduced if Covey wears a 'K9 the Safety Pup' costume and takes part in animal safety programs in elementary schools throughout New Jersey. Covey's girlfriend, Tiffany Duvall, had to be led from the courtroom in handcuffs when she began screaming that Covey's reduced sentence was not justice for the murder of her dog, Mr. Mimzy.

"Action News 10 in New Jersey has learned that Covey decided to accept the judge's offer 'because I love children,' he said. The problem is he loves children too much.

"Action 10 News in New Jersey has learned that Covey is registered under Megan's Law as a sex offender. Covey was overheard saying that the K9 the Safety Pup gig would 'help me bag some twelve-year-old.'

"Covey claimed later that he was referring to twelve-year-old scotch."

# 5

Travis Bodine felt like hearing the word of the gospel on this fine Sunday morning. And although it would never occur to him to actually attend church services, a God-fearing man knew that good Sunday morning preaching was never farther away than his old radio.

Travis slowly and carefully got up from his workbench and walked over to the shelf that held his autographed copies of *The Anarchist Cookbook* and *The Poor Man's James Bond*. He pushed the books aside and turned on the radio. It crackled and popped, and then there was lots of static. Travis leaned in, trying to hear the voice coming through.

*"Democrat Clinton Kendall and Republican challenger Pete Moreno are now in a neck-and-neck race to be New Jersey's next senator. Polls show the candidates in a dead heat with each getting forty-nine percent of the vote. . . . In other news, the annual New Jersey bear hunt is stirring up controversy again. . . ."*

"Shit," Travis said angrily, backing away from the radio's corrupted speaker. He didn't give a damn about the bears or the election. He knew there was no end to the corruption in New Jersey politics, so he didn't give a damn who won the

Senate race. It didn't matter. As far as he was concerned, Kendall and Moreno were both crooks.

Disgusted, Travis whacked the radio a few times, then fiddled with the dial until he heard the familiar voice of Brother Claude Dougherty. Travis smiled. He loved Brother Dougherty.

Dougherty ran his church services like a rock show. Sometimes Travis had seen Brother Dougherty, or "BD" as his congregation called him, on television. There were colored strobe lights flashing and electric guitar solos punctuating the hymns.

Travis could picture it now. Dougherty was a master showman.

He dug into his shirt pocket and pulled out a pack of Marlboros. He knocked one out, clamped it between his lips, then fired it up, fervently inhaling the smoke along with Brother Dougherty's fiery sermon.

*"The world is full of latter-day sinners, my dear friends in Christ. Fornicators! Adulterers! Sodomites! We are on a one-way trip to eternal damnation, brothers and sisters. It is time for the righteous among us to stand up. Stand up and make a blood atonement! Stand up and choose salvation! It is our time. It is time to do the Lord's work. The Lord cares more for one righteous man than for one million of the ungodly! Can I preach it like I feel it?*

*"Yes, Brother Claude, preach it!!*

*"I know the elections are near, my friends, and politics will force you to choose one side or the other. But on this Sunday, before we exercise our right, I will not stand here and endorse either candidate, but remember, before you are a Democrat or a Republican, you are a Christ-o-crat, or a member of the G.O.P.—God's Only Party. You are not going to get into heaven. You have to be a righteous man first. Can I get an Amen?"*

"Amen to that, Brother Claude," Travis said softly as he walked back to his workbench.

Travis Bodine was one righteous man. He had done time in a federal penitentiary for not paying his income taxes and for beating the crap out of the IRS agent who discovered that he hadn't.

When Travis was released, he found religion. He cleansed his soul. The next thing he did was learn everything he could about explosives and weapons.

Travis took to these skills easily, as if his talents were God-given. He swore on God's holy name to kill anyone who ever tried to make him pay taxes again.

Apparently, the anger-management classes he had been forced to take as a condition of his probation hadn't sunk in. He still preferred to handle his anger in his own unique and combustible way.

Travis knew that God was angry, too. There was evidence of His fury everywhere. That's why He sent wars, suicide bombers, tsunamis, and hurricanes. Travis blamed the U.S. government for allowing the sinners to flourish under its protection.

*". . . Here in this sanctified place, and to those of you out there watching and listening to our broadcast, let us confess our sins so that we may obtain forgiveness by His infinite goodness and mercy. Let us kneel with penitent hearts and confess our sins. Let us hold on to His hand. Let us pray that He rids us of abortionists! That He rids us of homosexuals! That He rids us of parlors of death and dens of flesh and debasement!"*

"And taxes!" Travis yelled to Brother Claude. "Don't forget the taxes. May He rid us of taxes!"

Travis's government had failed him. That's why God sent him to get revenge.

So far, he had taken God's revenge to two post offices and a federal construction site. Travis didn't know why God had sent the tsunami, didn't know what the people of Phi Phi Island had done to incur his wrath, but the place was filled with little brown-skinned people, so they must have been up to something.

Looking into the briefcase on his workbench, Travis made a final inspection of the C-4 plastic explosive inside it. He cut along the seams of a lead-lined photography bag used to protect newly shot film and fashioned it to fit over the mechanics of the wiring and detonator to avoid detection. Then he closed the false bottom and filled the rest of the briefcase with paper clips, pushpins, pencils, pens, a calculator, and other objects one would ordinarily find in a briefcase. He added as much as he could. It was all good for shrapnel after the bomb exploded.

Travis could have easily used a car or truck bomb parked in the bottom of the federal building, but he loved getting up close. Loved getting in the government's face. The briefcase bombs were perfect for him. His weapon of choice. His signature sedition.

Sitting back, he mentally played out his next moves. The timing had to be perfect. He would take the bomb to the IRS building in Newark. The briefcase would pass undetected through the scanner.

He would then take the elevator to the cafeteria on the eighth floor, where he would leave the briefcase somewhere inconspicuously. Take the elevator back down. Exit the building, and watch the explosion from another nearby location.

"KA-fucking-BOOM!" Travis whooped. *'Scuse me, Jesus.*

Travis could visualize it all so clearly. There would be a bright orange explosion, followed by yelling people fleeing from the building, pointing upward.

There would be screams coming from the place where

some would be trapped. Incredible sounds of wild desperate fear. Death and destruction everywhere. Lots of debris clattering to the sidewalk. A splintered table here. A mangled tray cabinet there. Thick black smoke rising up into the mid-morning Monday sky.

A clamor of fire alarms and sirens shrieking warnings.

That would shake those fat, lazy, income-taxing federal employees from their eight-hour coffee break.

Travis picked up his work knife and traced the letters he had carved into his palms after he was released from prison. SOG. He did it again. This time taking the knife deeper. SOG. Soldier of God. His palms started to bleed.

On the radio, Brother Dougherty shouted, *"We need the faithful to be unafraid to take a stand for Jesus!! We need a Christ explosion!!"*

And as Brother Dougherty's choir started to sing, Travis lifted his palms, offering his blood atonement and sang along.

> *"He's got the whole world in His hands.*
> *He's got the whole world in His hands.*
> *He's got the whole world in His hands.*
> *He's got the whole world in His hands."*

Time to do the Lord's work.

Travis shut the briefcase and gave a loud rebel yell.

# 6

One block over, on the top floor of a deserted home, two agents were observing Bodine through telescopes. It was the sixteenth consecutive day of watching him. They had lived in the home without leaving for a minute. They were paid to notice patterns, learn routines. The room was littered with stained, empty coffee cups and old pizza boxes.

The morning started out like every other day.

The target got up went into the bathroom

"Time?" the first agent asked.

"Seven forty-eight."

"The target is in the bathroom."

The second agent wrote it down. They were the same notes he had taken every day for over two weeks.

"The target is exiting the bathroom and going into the kitchen."

"Breakfast," the second agent said, and yawned. "I'll bet he has the same thing for breakfast he always has."

The agent with the telescope didn't take the bet. Bodine did the same thing every morning. He drank a Budweiser and smoked a cigarette. That was breakfast.

But then he did something different. He went into his work area. When he started working on the briefcase, the men snapped to attention and rapidly started taking notes and pictures. They captured every detail of the briefcase and its contents.

They watched and recorded as he turned on his radio. The first agent adjusted his headphones and checked the input levels on the recording system. All systems were go. The microphones were functioning flawlessly, and the audio feed was crystal clear.

When Bodine picked up the knife and cut himself, the first agent took out his cell phone and dialed.

The phone at the other end rang three times before it was picked up.

No one on the other end spoke.

"Get me Aster," the agent said urgently.

"He's in a meeting."

"This is Team Leader One. Goddammit, put me through."

The agent heard the anonymous voice at the other end say, "I think you better take this call."

Seconds later, "This is Aster."

"Commander, the target is getting ready to make his move."

# 7

Slick woke up and stretched. She walked into the bathroom, and when she was done, she washed her hands and splashed some water on her face.

The sun was coming in the widows. Laura was still asleep. Garbo was on the foot of the bed wagging her tail, paws in the air, ready for her walk.

Slick threw on some sweats and socks, then did some warm-up exercises. She dropped to the floor and did thirty push-ups, followed by thirty sit-ups as quietly as she could with Garbo licking her face and occasionally pulling on her socks. When she finally opened the bedroom door, Garbo excitedly ran out before her.

Once outside, Slick let the warm Sunday morning sunshine spill over her. Garbo romped and chased birds and squirrels and in between did what she needed to do. Slick walked to the end of the property and picked up the Sunday *Star Ledger* and read the headlines.

Garbo wanted to play, so Slick put the paper down and tossed a ball for her to fetch until she was no longer interested in the game.

Then she walked back to the house, opened the door, and walked up the stairs to the bedroom, with Garbo close on her heels.

She opened the bedroom door. Laura was awake and watching television. Charles Osgood was describing what was coming up on *Sunday Morning*.

Slick put the paper on the bed and kissed Laura.

"Good morning," Laura said.

"Good morning."

"Someone's had a workout already."

"Sorry," Slick apologized. "I didn't mean to get my sweat on you."

"I don't mind at all. What's it like outside?"

"It's beautiful. I say we go for a long walk in the mountains later."

"That sounds great," Laura said. "I'd love to."

"What's Charles up to today?" Slick asked, pointing to the television.

"There're going to be stories on Stevie Nicks and Vanessa Redgrave. Stevie has a new CD coming out, and Vanessa has a one-woman show opening on Broadway."

Laura slid over to make room in the bed for Slick.

It was their Sunday morning ritual: read the paper in bed and watch the Sunday talk shows. They would start with *Sunday Morning*, switch to *The Chris Matthews Show*, watch *Meet the Press,* and finish with *The McLaughlin Group.*

They would discuss and argue every show, take a long hot shower together, then have brunch. Sunday was their favorite day of the week.

They had just assumed their Sunday morning positions—Laura propped up on the pillows watching television with Garbo in her lap, Slick prone on the bed leafing through the

"Parade" section of the newspaper—when Slick's cell phone rang.

"Hello."

The voice on the other end drew her full attention.

"Yes, sir," she said. "We're looking forward to it."

Laura knew without asking.

Slick clicked off her cell.

"That was the official word. We go as planned. Tomorrow."

"I'm ready," Laura said.

"I'll go make coffee," said Slick. "Then we can go over the information I just got."

Laura picked up the remote and clicked off Charles Osgood, then sighed.

This Sunday morning was definitely headed in a different direction.

# 8

At eleven thirty-eight Monday morning, Travis Bodine was
fourth in line to enter the Jonathan C. Dooley IRS building
at Newark's Federal Plaza. He put his briefcase on the conveyor belt to get X-rayed and stepped through the metal de-
tector. There were no alarms or buzzers.

The gorgeous blond security guard who handed the
briefcase back to him smiled and said, "Have a good day."

Travis let his hand linger on hers. The heat coming
from her was like a blast furnace. He could almost taste the
heat.

When he took the case from her, he could see the smile
fade, but something warm stayed in her eyes.

Travis started toward the elevator but looked back at the
blonde. She was busy with other items on the conveyor belt.

Travis looked at her ass. It was a great ass, supported by
long shapely legs.

It was an ass a God-fearing man could fall down on his
knees and worship. He felt a twitching in his stomach, and
lower. He'd love to plunge himself into that ass, get lost in it.

Riding her while she screamed. Making her born again. And again and again.

Travis whistled softly and sincerely hoped she took her lunch break away from the building. He looked at his watch. The bomb would go off in a half hour. He walked to the elevator and pushed the UP button. The doors opened; no one was inside, and no one got in with him. The doors were about to close when a cane stopped them.

A blind black woman tapped her way in, led by the smallest seeing-eye dog Travis had ever seen. What the hell kind of freaky little poofy dog was that, anyway?

He felt momentarily unsure, then let it go. The woman was blind, after all. She felt the braille buttons and pushed number nine.

The elevator started to rise.

The little dog started to sniff the briefcase; then it grabbed hold of Travis's pant leg and wouldn't let go. The dog wasn't being hostile. It held on playfully, like it would a favorite old sock.

Annoyed, he could have easily kicked the dog away but decided against it. He didn't want to attract more attention to himself.

Maybe this black bitch would survive the blast, and even though she was blind, he didn't want to give her more to remember.

He remained focused on why he was there and tolerated the little mutt. Maybe the anger-management course had done some good after all.

The black woman tried to stop the dog but couldn't make it let go of Travis's leg.

"Bad girl," she kept saying over and over in between apologies.

The elevator made its way up, passing the second, third, fourth, and fifth floors without taking on any other passengers.

When the elevator reached the sixth floor, it stopped suddenly with a bounce and a thud, and then all the lights went out. They were enveloped in darkness.

The only relief was a dim margin of light that filtered in somehow from above the elevator car.

"What's happening?" the blind woman asked nervously. Her dog started to get agitated and began growling in the dark.

"Power failure," Travis answered tersely. He cursed himself for not having thought of this possibility.

Travis stayed calm. He looked at his watch. Ten minutes remained before the detonator would engage.

Several moments passed. Travis could feel the time slipping away.

The woman became increasingly frantic. The dog was now barking excitedly. She picked it up to calm it down and held it close.

They all stayed silent in the darkness.

*Tick, tick, tick . . .*

"What's taking so long?" she asked eventually. "Why isn't someone coming for us?"

Travis started to assess his terrible reality. The briefcase was going to explode soon, and he knew with breath-crushing certainty he was going to die. He began to feel fevered. Panic was taking hold of him. His mind was unraveling. His heart was jackhammering.

He lunged for the elevator operating panel, pushing the buttons like mad, trying to get the elevator started again; then he tried the emergency phone.

It was dead.

"What are you doing?" the blind woman screamed.

"I've got to get out of here." Travis had started to cry.

He was pounding furiously on the elevator doors. "I've got a bomb. It's going to explode."

"What!" the woman yelled at him.

"My briefcase! It's a bomb!"

"What! You made a bomb and brought it here?"

"Yes! Yes, I did," Travis slobbered through his tears. "Jesus help me! I've got to get out of here."

Sweat ran down the back of his neck, across his forehead, and from his underarms down the length of his sides. His knees began to feel like they would soon fold.

Slick removed her sunglasses and smiled. "That sounds like a confession to me."

She walked to the elevator security camera and said, "I hope you guys got all of that."

Travis turned to look at her in disbelief. "Who the hell are you?"

"I'm a detective. And you've just confessed to trying to bomb a federal building. But dry your eyes there, Firecracker. The bomb squad is standing by just on the other side of those doors."

Slick addressed the camera again. "Okay. He's confessed. You can let us out now."

The elevator didn't move. The doors didn't open.

Slick pounded hard on the walls. "Let us out. NOW."

Nothing happened.

Slick picked up the elevator phone. "Oh, my God. This really isn't working."

Travis saw her frown with concern. There was fear in her eyes, and he knew something was very wrong.

Slick remembered Laura's concern that she would make a mistake.

"How much time would you say is left?" Slick asked hoarsely.

Travis looked at his watch.

"About eight minutes."

"OH, SHIT!" Slick shouted, and started to pound wildly on the doors. Travis started to pound with her.

They tried uselessly to pry the doors apart and yelled at the top of their lungs for help. Their desperate pounding and raw shouts went unheard and did nothing but blast back from the steel walls and echo in the elevator.

They stopped yelling, accepting that it was useless. The motionlessness was maddening.

Travis looked back in nauseated horror at the briefcase. The blood drained from his face. His bowels let loose just as the briefcase exploded.

*KA–BOOM!*

The briefcase erupted with a resounding roar. Confetti blasted from its insides and flurried down. Then Travis passed out.

Slick made sure Garbo was okay. The dog's stubby little tail was wagging happily as she leapt at the confetti, trying to catch it. Slick brushed the confetti from her hair and clothes.

"*Now* will you let me out of here?" Slick asked loudly. "Bodine just dropped a stink bomb. Tell Laura I trust her with my life, and tell Sam he owes me one hundred dollars. I knew this weasel would lose it if he got a taste of his own medicine."

"We're on our way," Slick heard through the tiny receiver in her ear.

"Good job. Very good job." The man speaking on the other end of the receiver sounded pleased.

Forty-five minutes later, the Newark police were taking Travis Bodine, stinking, spent, and hyperventilating, into custody. As he was driven away, he saw the blind black woman from the elevator and the gorgeous blond security guard, smiling at him and waving good-bye.

It took a few seconds, but Travis Bodine realized what had happened to him. These two bitches had taken him down. He became enraged. He couldn't beat on the window of the cruiser, because his hands were cuffed, so he started head-butting the window and cursing them.

"Bitches! Bitches! Fucking bitches! I'll kill you! I'll kill you!"

The officer sitting in the back loved it. He was waiting for an opportunity. With great pleasure he Tasered Travis, who folded like a lawn chair.

The cruiser was silent again.

When he was gone from sight, Laura said to Slick, "I thought for sure he'd notice that I switched the briefcases."

"I knew for sure he'd be too busy noticing you," Slick said, winking at her. "You were perfect, Laura. I knew you would be. I remembered how scared you were that you'd make a mistake. I knew you wouldn't. You've got to learn to trust yourself as much as I trust you."

Slick kissed her on the cheek.

"I'm just glad it's over," Laura said, closing her eyes, leaning in and enjoying having her cheek kissed.

The receiver in Slick's ear began to crackle.

"We're still watching you."

Slick laughed.

"Nice working with you, Commander," she answered back. She wondered where he was. He could see and hear her every move, but Slick had no idea from where he was observing her.

"Congratulations on a very successful operation," the commander said. "You helped avert a crisis and capture a dangerous man who was on the way to becoming an even more serious threat. Now his ass is ours. We'll take real good care of Bodine from here."

"I'm sure you will, sir."

Travis had been arrested by the Newark police, but after they were through with him, he'd be turned over to the Feds. The Feds didn't like terrorists who tried to blow up federal buildings.

The receiver in her ear crackled one last time. She knew the connection was being broken and that it would be untraceable.

Slick pulled it out of her ear, threw it into the street as she had been instructed, and watched as a taxi ran over it, smashing it into useless pieces.

Smiling, she looked up to the roofs of the surrounding buildings, and the sharpshooters who had camped out there since midnight were giving them a thumbs-up.

Slick and Laura nodded surreptitiously so as not to give away their positions.

On the street, a dirty, rusted-out van with ST. MARK'S HOME-LESS SHELTER printed on the side pulled up. The van lacked a rear bumper, and the passenger side window was mostly duct tape. The engine, however, maintained a steady healthy rumble. The Critical Incident team that had been stationed on the ground disguised as drunks and street people disappeared inside the vehicle.

The van pulled away and disappeared into the morning. No one on the street even seemed to notice. It was as if they were never there.

By the time Slick and Laura looked back up, the rooftops that had been speckled with dozens of men looking through rifle scopes had been cleared, too. Slick had heard the commander once refer to them as Alpha Team. They were probably getting ready for their next mission.

A major disaster had been avoided quietly and professionally, without panic. And there would never be a news story or report about it. No one would recognize Alpha Team for the heroes they were.

Perfect. That was just the way they wanted it.

"Damn, those guys are good," Slick said with admiration.

Garbo stood on her hind legs, demanding Slick's attention.

"Yes, little girl. You were wonderful, too. You kept Bodine distracted after Laura switched the briefcase."

Slick bent down to give Garbo a biscuit, and the three of them started across the street. Slick stopped at a *Star Ledger* vending machine, bought a paper, and read the headline.

**NEW JERSEY SENATORIAL RACE HEATS UP**

Nothing like New Jersey politics, she thought. Slick drew in a long deep breath. "Let's go home," she said.

"Let's," Laura agreed. "We've got some shopping and packing to do for our vacation."

They started walking to Slick's car, a Mercedes SLK350 with a sticker on the window announcing that she was a retired police officer, a gift from one of her pals on the job that prevented her from being ticketed for any but the most flagrant parking violations.

It also kept would-be car thieves away. They saw the sticker and decided it was a bad idea to steal an ex-cop's car.

In the distance, a police car with its siren blaring approached. It snaked and zigzagged its way through the heavy midmorning traffic.

One by one, drivers swerved reflexively to let it pass.

Slick and Laura looked startled as it stopped in front of them.

A young police officer got out of the car. "Detective Slick?"

After years off the force, the police still addressed her as "Detective" out of respect. And after all these years, Slick still cherished hearing it.

"Yes, Officer. How can I help you?"

"Captain DeStasio sent us to bring you to the station."

Slick started to ask why her old precinct captain would be sending for her, but before she could ask, the young officer continued. "All I can tell you, Detective, is that it's about a murder. Some Halsey Street hooker went and got herself killed."

The young officer hesitated and looked away momentarily, then finished. His youthful voice was low and strained. "Could be someone on the job is involved."

Without saying another word, Slick opened the back

door of the patrol car and helped Laura and Garbo inside. She walked to the other side and let herself in.

The car worked its way back into traffic with the lights flashing and the siren screaming.

Inside the car was total silence. No one spoke.

Slick did a quick study of the young officer in the front seat. His appearance was impeccable. Uniform clean and crisp. Hair cut to regulation. Great physical condition. His eyes were forward and focused. He hadn't expected to work in Newark, but when he got the assignment, he didn't turn it down, because he thought he could make a difference. He argued with his young wife about it. She wanted kids, a house at the shore.

He was doing his job, but it was easy to see he was despondent. He hadn't heard that sometimes the cops were suspected of being the bad guys.

Yeah, he knew about Abner Louima and Amadou Diallo, but those were not the norm for police officers. Those incidents were aberrations.

He was probably fresh out of the academy, Slick thought, filled with the rookie's altruistic ideal that the cops were always right and good.

He couldn't believe that the people he worked with could be guilty of anything more than taking a free meal from a restaurant once in a while.

Slick knew exactly how he felt. She looked out the window at the same old Newark streets that she remembered so well.

Halsey Street.

Broad Street.

Frelinghuysen Avenue.

Ferry Street.

The movie theaters, the barbecue joints, the check-cashing places, the jazz clubs.

The squad car seemed to be carrying Slick swiftly into her past.

She shut her eyes, remembering how she had gotten this far and the first time she saw a police badge.

# 9

If New Jersey is the Garden State, then Newark is the hole where the serpent dwells. Hot humid summers with reeking garbage. Icy winter winds that blasted up the streets and continued unmercifully until the city was frozen solid.

And in the spring when the promise of renewed life was evident throughout the rest of New Jersey, in Newark the sun remained distant and diffused behind low-hanging clouds, making the downtown cityscape dreary and gray, heightening the pervading aura of collapse.

Crowded. Cheerless. Deteriorating. Violent.

Some families hang on together and survive life in Newark. Others lose their grip and don't.

The third and last child born into Marvin and Estelle Slick's family was a strangely self-possessed little girl they named Cassandra.

Estelle would often tell the story about how moments after her birth, Cassandra gave her a cryptic smile. Though her eyes were closed, the power of that smile was astounding.

If ever a child was blessed with a confident spirit, this one was already exuberant with it.

The baby was unexpected but not unwelcome.

Marvin and Estelle had been planning to use the meager savings they managed to scrape together over the years to move their family out of their weather-beaten two-story home in Newark. But with the arrival of Cassandra, the move was impossible.

So they stayed in their sorry home with the grime-coated windows and the front porch that had started to crumble and sag to the left, and did the best they could.

Marvin worked full-time during the day as a manager of a security guard firm. Then after Cassandra's birth, he took a second job driving a cab at night and on weekends.

He knew he would never be able to give his family the best of everything, but he would give them what they needed and see that his kids got a good education so they could get themselves out of Newark. His children would make a better life for their children.

Marvin and Estelle gladly made room in their hearts and their home for their only daughter. They made their family's clothes last as long as possible, they ate macaroni three times a week, and they strained for years to watch the few fuzzy channels they got on their outmoded television set.

They never discussed that they were poor in front of their children. They never complained about what they didn't have. When they took their family to church on Sundays, they gave thanks to the Lord for His many blessings.

It soon became very apparent to Marvin and Estelle that Cassandra was different from her older brothers and very different from themselves. In fact, there were no similarities at all.

At times, Marvin and Estelle privately looked at each other suspiciously, each wondering what secret family genetic defect the other carried but had failed to mention that had produced this alien offspring.

At times, they felt an odd mixture of pride and embarrassment because Cassandra was so different, so strange, sometimes bordering on weird.

When baby Cassandra started talking after nine months, it was without the slightest hint of baby-speak. Marvin and Estelle hovered over her, coaxing her, eagerly anticipating her first uttered "Mama" and "Dada."

Instead, Cassandra's first words were "George Washington, John Adams, Thomas Jefferson . . ." Her parents' jaws dropped as they heard Cassandra list all the U.S. presidents in order.

When she then proceeded to name the states and their capitals, Marvin and Estelle were speechless.

Estelle had propped Cassandra up in her play swing in front of the TV set for hours, tuned to the PBS channel, whenever she did her housework.

Cassandra watched and absorbed everything like a sponge. She was hungry for information with an overload of curiosity.

After witnessing her ability to retain and process any and all information, Estelle was very grateful she hadn't left the TV channel on a soap opera or some salacious talk show. The poor child would have learned a hundred ways to be dysfunctional before she had even reached one year.

By age two, Cassandra was reading the newspaper. And she wasn't just reading the words. She understood them. Every day she would wait for the paper by the door, sitting on her little Fisher-Price motorcycle, eager for it to be delivered.

When it came, she would grab it, then pedal like mad into her bedroom, sometimes knocking down her brothers.

"Out of my way, siblings" was all they heard as she streaked by.

Cassandra would spread the paper on her little bed and read the crime section to her turtle Aretha and her two goldfish, whom she sometimes called Leopold and Loeb or Starsky and Hutch, depending on her mood. She would do this until *Sesame Street* started.

By age four, she had mastered the Rubik's Cube and every other word game or puzzle her parents put in front of her.

She could figure out the ending to TV shows and movies well before the rest of the family. Her favorite shows were *Get Christy Love* and *Charlie's Angels.* She would pretend she was Pam Grier in *Coffy* and *Foxy Brown,* often trying to kick the butts of her poor long-suffering older brothers.

"Take that, you jive turkey!" Cassandra would pounce on them from out of nowhere.

Her brothers would sigh and silently endure her barrage of karate chops and jabs.

They, of course, would never hit their little sister, no matter how tempting the prospect.

What Marvin and Estelle couldn't grasp was that, despite the genius of the riveting intricately written stories, Cassandra wasn't addicted to these dramas featuring female crime fighters. Something else entirely was going on.

Cassandra had collected a complete set of *Charlie's Angels* plates and glasses. She would drink from the Kate Jackson and Jaclyn Smith glasses interchangeably, without a fuss, but she absolutely insisted that all her meals be served only on a Farrah Fawcett plate.

Years later, when Cassandra told her parents that she was gay, Estelle looked back on this Farrah fixation as a missed clue.

And like the Angels, Christy Love, and Pam Grier, little

Cassandra felt she needed a car to be a more effective Super Chick. She had grown tired of her Fisher-Price motorcycle.

So one day she started the family car with a screwdriver and backed it across the street into their neighbors' car. Horns honked and brakes squealed as she peeled out of the driveway.

Frightened passersby dove for cover. Marvin and Estelle were forced to padlock all the tools after that.

From the time Cassandra started talking, her favorite thing was to ask, "Why?"

"Why are oranges round?"

"Why aren't there any eggs in an eggplant?"

"Why can't I jump off the roof?"

Her parents would tell her to do something, and Cassandra would look at them and ask, "Why?" It was always her first response. It drove them crazy.

At first Marvin and Estelle would give her a reason why, and then Cassandra would counter with at least six logical reasons to support her opposing view.

It was aggravating trying to debate a four-year-old. It was hard to stay mature and modulated. Especially when they could see that Cassandra delighted in knocking down their answers, always getting that I-can-keep-this-argument-going-for-hours look in her eyes.

Then she would go into fits of convulsive laughter as their frustration mounted and they ran out of reasons. They wanted to shake her until her hair rattled.

Cassandra challenged them on everything.

"For the last time, Cassandra, it is *not* toxic nuclear waste! Now eat your oatmeal, you hear me?"

"Stop stallin' and get your behind in that tub. You checked

three times already, you know there ain't no sharks in the bathwater."

"Your 'secret potion' to make yourself invisible didn't work. We can still see you. Put the ice cream back in the freezer and go put your clothes back on. NOW!"

"It's just a vaccination, not truth serum. No one's trying to drag a confession out of you—but when we get home, young lady, I want to know all about what you got to confess."

"Call this a dictatorship all you want. Take your butt to bed right now, missy, and stop calling me 'Mein Fuhrer,' and quit that goose-steppin'."

Damn that PBS!

Eventually, Marvin and Estelle simply said, "Because I told you to do it, and I'm the parent." It was the only response they could give that didn't lead to an argument. The because-I'm-the-parent card was played often. But once in a while, it led to more questions.

"Why are you my parents? Oh, really. Can you prove it, or am I just supposed to take your word for it? Do you have documentation? I need to see some hard evidence."

Cassandra wasn't a bad child, but when she misbehaved and her parents handed out punishment, she swore that she was a victim of a miscarriage of justice.

First she would demand legal representation. Then she would remind them of her civil liberties as an American citizen and threaten to call the Division of Youth and Family Services.

"Why are you so sure I was the one who broke the lamp?"

"Why can't I get a presidential pardon?"

"Why are you taking more aspirin?"

"Why are you sending me to my room?"

Marvin and Estelle couldn't wait for her to enter kindergarten, hoping school would feed and manage her intelligence, although Estelle felt a little guilty about what she was preparing to unleash on an unsuspecting school system.

Every night, Estelle prayed that her odd duck would somehow find her place in life. She turned Cassandra's life over to God, to do with as he saw fit. She thought he must have some very special plan for her that Estelle could not understand yet.

Marvin just prayed that the "sugar and spice and everything nice, that's what little girls are made of" thing would kick in eventually. It never did.

Cassandra excelled at school but did not make friends easily. Usually she sat alone quietly eating her PB&J-on-Wonder-Bread sandwiches at lunchtime.

It took years for her to finally make a true friend. When she did, she was very loyal and protective. Cassandra's friend would stand at Cassandra's back door and yell, "C'mon out and play, Cassie! C'mon! Hurry up, hurry up, hurry up!" And off they would go.

It was a private world, just big enough for Cassandra and her friend. They openly shared their thoughts and kept each other's secrets.

Her friend was the only one who understood Cassandra's unpredictable melancholy streak. She'd go quiet and drift off into her own thoughts.

But when class was in session, nothing could shut her up. She'd plant herself in the front row and raise her hand to answer every question. There was no stopping her inquisitiveness.

It was the same thing year after year as she went through elementary school. The other students would take uncontested notes based on the blind faith they had in their teachers.

Not Cassandra. She challenged every lesson with an urgent and passionate rebuttal.

Frequently, messages were sent home to Marvin and Estelle, requesting parent-teacher conferences. They averaged about five such requests a month.

Estelle had two sons before Cassandra. She could not be deceived anymore by the chummy informality of the notes. She knew that notes from school were written in code. A code buried so cunningly in the text that it could only be deciphered by a CIA code breaker or very concerned parents.

The word *parents,* for example, always meant they really wanted to speak to the mother. Marvin attended when he could, but usually it was Estelle who went to the parent-teacher conferences.

Most of the time, as she walked the halls of the school alone, none of the other parents would speak to her, but often they would look at her sympathetically, and Estelle would hear them whispering things like "That's the little Slick girl's mother. There but for the grace of God! She's really got a handful with that child" when they thought she was out of earshot.

At one of these conferences, Cassandra's second-grade teacher, Mrs. Truesdale, told Estelle that because of Cassandra, she had started smoking again. Two packs a day. Unfiltered.

Mrs. Downing, Cassandra's third-grade teacher, confided that since Cassandra became one of her students, she kept a small flask in her desk drawer. It was filled with Maalox. She took a few chugs from it daily and wondered if there was a twelve-step program for Maalox addicts.

Marvin and Estelle got a note from Cassandra's fourth-grade teacher, Mrs. Voorhees, requesting a meeting because "Cassandra is a very competitive little girl who will need to learn to lose more gracefully." But, before they could meet with her, Mrs. Voorhees was ordered to take time off from school after having developed a grotesque nervous tic that badly frightened the children.

After that, when Estelle prayed for her daughter, she always said a few kind words for her teachers, too.

When Cassandra was in fifth grade, Estelle would take her to the park on Sundays to let her run around and let Marvin sleep in late. One day, Cassandra wandered over to the picnic tables and watched the old men playing chess, fascinated.

She was hypnotized by the pieces and their movements. It excited her hungry mind. This game had everything. Concentration. Critical thinking. Pattern recognition. Strategic planning. Analysis. Maneuvering toward an ultimate goal.

It was the first time Estelle had ever seen her so challenged.

Cassandra loved the logic of the game. It made her mind focus.

Going to the park became a regular routine. When school was out for the summer, Cassandra was at the park every day.

At first, the old men thought it was cute that the pretty little girl with the big brown eyes would watch them play, so intrigued by their every move. The day she asked one of them for a game, the old men laughed and let her sit in. She won. After that, she won every game she played.

The regular chess players took her on one by one, and one by one they all lost.

After a while, some refused to play with her, and others would just pack up their boards and pieces when they saw her approaching.

Not wanting to lose the beneficial effects the game had

on Cassandra, Estelle learned how to play and convinced her
sons to learn to play, too. They did so reluctantly. They knew
they couldn't win. Cassandra crushed them every time.

On a hot night late that August, while Estelle and Cassandra
were home playing a game of chess, they heard a loud gunshot.
That was not unusual. Everyone on the block was used to
hearing gunshots from time to time. It was almost a weekend
ritual. Guns were either used for committing a crime or for
protection against one.

Estelle had never heard one so close to her home, though.
She carefully looked out the window and realized it came
from next door. She and Cassandra were alone in the house.
Marvin was working and the boys were at a baseball game.

Estelle slowly opened the door to see what was going on.
Cassandra stood close by, her curiosity kicking into high gear.

Mrs. Cleveland was in the middle of the street screaming
for someone to call an ambulance. Her phone service had
been shut off weeks before for lack of payment. She was almost incoherent, shrieking and babbling about how her husband had been cleaning his gun when it accidentally went
off.

Estelle and some of the other neighbors instinctively went
to Mrs. Cleveland to offer solace, and others ran for help. It
seemed like the whole block was up and out on the street.

In the confusion, no one noticed Cassandra enter the
Cleveland house.

An ambulance and two police cars arrived. While two officers tried to calm the neighbors and extract information,
the ambulance men and the two other officers started up the
stoop to enter the Cleveland house. Estelle had her arm
around Mrs. Cleveland to help her up the steps.

On the top step stood little Cassandra.

"Why did you shoot your husband, Mrs. Cleveland?" she asked.

"Cassandra!" Estelle was horrified. Mrs. Cleveland fainted. The police ran into the house.

Two weeks later, one of the officers who had been on duty that night stopped by to see Marvin and Estelle. He told them that Mr. Cleveland's death was indeed a homicide and not an accident. He turned to little Cassandra and handed her a little tin detective badge.

"Good job, Officer Slick," he said.

He stood at attention and saluted her. Then he shook her hand and told her the police force could use her when she grew up.

Cassandra Slick still has that badge tucked away. She had it in her pocket the day she graduated with honors from Howard University on a full scholarship, and she had it on the day she was sworn in as a police officer.

On that long-ago night, when Cassandra was first given that little tin badge, Estelle said her prayers and thanked the Lord for letting her know that her only daughter was going to be just fine.

Shortly after that, when the next pledge drive rolled around, Marvin and Estelle gratefully sent PBS a check for fifty dollars.


"Detective?"

From far away, the young officer's voice broke into her thoughts. She looked for him in the front seat, but the seat was empty.

"We're here, Detective," he said.

Slick had been so preoccupied with her memories that she hadn't noticed the car had stopped in front of the precinct house, and the officer was now holding the door open for her. Laura was standing on the sidewalk looking at her with concern. Slick nodded and exited the vehicle quietly. She stood for a moment and looked at the building she had entered hundreds of times before. But never before had her stomach muscles knotted up as they did at this moment.

# 10

Captain Frank DeStasio wasn't an unusually tall man, but everyone always felt small when standing next to him. He had a big wide chest and muscular arms, and he created the impression of a man perfectly balanced, impossible to rush, fluster, or inflame. His once-golden locks had thinned and fled. What was left was closely cropped and shot through with gray.

His features were large and well formed: strong nose, jutting jaw, full lips, broad forehead. He had the shrewd eyes of an experienced gambler. He knew when to take risks and when not to. His was a face that projected strength, cunning, dignity, and intelligence. The face of a man born to command.

DeStasio had been a Marine before joining the department. Everything he did on the job was disciplined and right to the point—every word, every gesture, every glance. His brown suit and olive-green tie resembled the uniform he had worn for years as a Marine. He took to police work immediately.

The job claimed him for life the moment he joined the

force. He had worked in Newark as a patrol officer, then moved to NYC, where he became a detective. He came back to New Jersey, then landed the captain's position at his old precinct in Newark.

The office walls were filled with plaques and pictures, tokens of a long career that had brought its share of recognition. Behind his desk, framed by two American flags, was a large pre-9/11 photograph of the World Trade Center. The picture had been shot from ground level, and the towers rose, seemingly forever, white and pristine, into a flawless blue sky. It was a vivid silent reminder of friends and coworkers he had lost on that day as well as the ones who had quit shortly afterward. They had lost heart after that day. Who could blame them?

DeStasio was eligible for retirement; he had even gotten his paperwork done and ready to go, but he felt he couldn't leave. It was not the time to retire. It would feel like desertion.

So he stayed and hung that picture on his wall as a testimony to the respect he felt for police officers and the job. Since then, eight years had passed.

Captain DeStasio rose from his seat and walked over to the window that looked out onto Broad Street. He stared down at the endless traffic until he found what he was searching for. He watched with cool eyes as one of the best detectives he'd ever commanded exited the police car he had sent for her.

Looking down at her now, he couldn't recall if he'd ever told her she was one of his best. Her investigations, without exception, were quick, precise, clean, and contained. He needed her skills now.

Their respect for each other was mutual. But what he

wanted from her now would open up old wounds in her that had barely knit together. He hoped that in the end, their mutual respect would still be there. But even if it wasn't, it was a gamble he had to take.

The captain ran a catalog of possibilities through his mind as to how this meeting might go. Its success would depend on his knowledge of the two officers involved. He couldn't shake the feeling that he was about to find out truths about one of his officers he might not be ready for.

He poured himself a cup of coffee from the large pot on the table under the window and walked back to his desk. He sat down heavily in his chair and mustered his thoughts. And waited.

After about five minutes, there was a light tap at the door. "Come in."

DeStasio got up from his desk, extended his right hand to Slick, and rested his left hand on her shoulder. He was welcoming home a fellow soldier.

Laura saw nothing but respect in Slick's demeanor as she shook the hand of the man who had sent for her. Then she turned to Laura and said, "Captain, this is my partner, Laura Charles."

"Of course, I've heard of you, Miss Charles. It's a pleasure to finally meet you."

"It's Laura, please. And the pleasure is all mine."

There were three chairs set up in front of the captain's desk. Slick sat down in the middle chair so that she was directly in front of the captain's desk, and Laura sat to her right. Garbo lay down on the floor between them.

Captain DeStasio offered them coffee, which they both declined.

"I see you and Laura have been keeping yourselves busy, Slick," the captain began. "I heard about the murders at that community theater in South Orange and the kidnapping in Bernardsville. Wasn't there something, too, in . . . Atlantic City, right?" he asked.

"Yes. Some guys were trying to simultaneously rob three casinos one night during Neil Diamond's show at the Tropicana."

"I guess Crackling Rosie's still got her sizzle, eh? Are you a Neil Diamond fan?"

"I am not, said I. I am not, I cried."

The captain laughed.

"And today, the capture of the bomber in the IRS building. Only a few of us in the department knew that bomber thing was going down. How'd you get in on that job?"

"I'd been following his activities. I put together a profile of the guy and notified Homeland Security. Believe it or not, they got the Feds, the state, and the city to work together and call off the usual turf wars."

"You're kidding? A full-court press. That's no small miracle. It must have taken a lot of planning to anticipate Bodine's every move."

Slick shrugged it off like it was no big deal. "Like a good game of chess," she said.

"Good job, Detective. As always."

"Thank you, Captain."

Captain DeStasio took a deep breath, signaling the end of the small talk, then jumped right in. "The reason I called you back to the house today is because a prostitute's been murdered, and one of our own was using her as a snitch. Unofficially. She was never registered as a confidential informant."

Slick looked surprised. DeStasio had always done every-thing by the book. The department didn't allow unregistered CIs.

"I just found out about this," he continued. "I wasn't happy that the hooker wasn't on the books as a snitch, but I believe the officer involved had legitimate reasons not to do so. I reviewed some of the cases she gave tips on. She gave some good information."

"Then that's good enough for me. What can I do?"

"I'm sure you can appreciate that this is a very sensitive situation. The officer swears noninvolvement with the pross getting murdered, but I need you to look into it. Objectively. Guilty or innocent, I'll stand by whatever your investigation uncovers."

"I'm not sure I can be objective, Captain," Slick said hon-estly. "This is my old precinct, my home. I have lots of ties to the people here."

Slick was thinking about her former partner Sam Billings-ley, with whom she'd attended the police academy, and her good friends, Officers Cathy Simpson and Paula Rafferty. They had all logged in a lot of overtime here working on cases to-gether and watching out for each other. They were all openly gay at a time when it was difficult to be a gay cop.

Together they had organized a chapter of the Fraternal Order of Police for gay black officers that they affectionately called "The Homey-sexuals." They had been through a lot together. If any of them was in trouble now, Slick wanted to help.

"I'm here for you. I'll do whatever you want," she said. Her concern was genuine, her devotion to her former fellow officers almost palpable.

The captain took a long pause before he spoke. "The officer involved is Tom Brandeal."

Slick was instantly reminded of Travis Bodine. Because without warning, her former captain had just dropped a bomb on her.

*KA-BOOM!*

# 11

"Tom Brandeal? No fucking way. I'm outta here. I hope that racist, homophobic son of a bitch gets the needle." Slick spat the words out acidly, then shot up from her chair and started for the door. "Come on, Laura, let's go."

Before Laura could move, the captain called out, "Detective." The word stopped Slick at the door. Laura noticed that Captain DeStasio wasn't fazed by Slick's outburst. It was almost as if he had anticipated it. He didn't speak loudly, but he was firm.

"Your work after leaving the job still brings you in contact with a lot of police in a lot of different precincts. You have a great reputation, Slick. Cops cooperate with you whenever you ask. How do you think it's going to look when word gets around that your old boss reached out to you, and you refused to help a fellow officer?"

Slick turned away from the door and looked at her former commander incredulously.

"No, that's not a threat," DeStasio said, reading her thoughts. "I would never tell a soul about what was said here today. You got a lot of juice in the department, Slick. Cops will continue to cooperate with you no matter what you decide. But you know how the job works. You know how cops are. Some cops won't cooperate anymore if you refuse to help Brandeal, even if he is an asshole. Do you really want to take the chance of alienating cops? There's lots of gossip going around. Some folks already know Brandeal is in a jackpot. And they'll know almost as soon as you walk out that door that you refused to help him."

Slick couldn't believe what she was hearing, couldn't absorb what he was asking. More than anyone else, DeStasio knew the history she had with Tom Brandeal. Slick and Brandeal had competed twice for promotions. Slick had got them both.

Brandeal eventually made detective, but he still harbored bad feelings toward Slick. She had no patience for his open and well-known contempt for blacks and gays.

And, of course, there was the Sean MacGuire case that Slick and Brandeal had worked together. The case cut her deeply. She was sure Brandeal had planted evidence to get a conviction, sure MacGuire was innocent, but she had never been able to prove it and had never stopped wondering what more she could have done. Now Sean MacGuire was dead.

DeStasio looked at Slick now, and he could almost see the ghost that haunted her from that case float across her eyes. He could feel the chill of doubt that claimed a piece of her soul. The captain had a fleeting thought that he was asking a lot of her, maybe too much.

So DeStasio looked away quickly, but he did not stop. "Would you please just listen to what we know so far?" he asked. Slick said nothing. "Humor me, Detective," DeStasio said, applying pressure.

Slick still didn't answer but looked at Laura. The expression on Laura's face urged her to stay.

DeStasio opened the file on his desk and began to read. " 'The DOA, black female prostitute, in her early thirties, known by her street name, Paradise, was seen on Halsey Street on Friday night at approximately ten P.M. Later the same evening, the night clerk at the Garden State Motor Lodge on Route 22 in Hillside distinctly remembers seeing a black female matching Paradise's description check into the Lodge at eleven-thirty P.M. She came to the front desk and paid for the room. She was obnoxious and loud. It was just an overnight rental. The clerk says a man was with her, but the clerk did not get a good look at him, because he stayed outside.

" 'All he remembers is the big cowboy hat the man was wearing. And from the noise and laughter, they both appeared to have been drinking a lot.

" 'About an hour later, the clerk saw the man in the cowboy hat drive away alone. The next morning, the maid came in to clean the room. The room was destroyed. The bed was soaked with so much blood that the victim had to have died. And according to the maid, the hotel bedding was missing.

" 'Saturday night, the car that the clerk saw the man in the cowboy hat drive away in was found in Surprise Lake in Mountainside. Paradise's body was in the trunk, wrapped in bedding matching the maid's description. Broken neck, multiple stab wounds. Paradise has now been identified. We put a name to her—Gloria Roxley.' "

DeStasio closed the file and looked at Slick for her reaction.

At first she had no reaction, but eventually she asked, "Have you notified Internal Affairs about Brandeal?"

"That's procedure. His duties have been restricted. Brandeal is now working a desk job."

Then, without another word, set and determined, DeStasio extended the case file to her. After only a brief hesitation, Slick took the file from him and slowly leafed through its contents.

"Okay, I'll do it," she said, finally looking up.

There was a knock at the door, and before the captain could answer, in walked Tom Brandeal.

"I was told to come see you . . ." He stopped midsentence when he realized the captain wasn't alone and just who was in his office.

Slick and Brandeal took steps toward each other, then stopped, like two boxers meeting at center ring, staring each other down. For a long moment, neither of them moved. The hostility was tangible.

Then Brandeal moved in closer, getting in Slick's face. He grinned broadly, condescendingly. "Well, well, well. What a pleasant surprise. It's Shaft's little sister, Shtick."

"I'm fighting back an ocean of tears, Brandeal. Nothing stings quite like a pun," Slick said. She stepped in closer to him. "I see you've progressed from merely planting evidence, Brandeal, to prime suspect in a murder. That's a real step up for you. It shows progress in your personal growth. And I used to think you were such a dedicated underachiever."

Brandeal backed up a step as the situation started to sink in. He saw the file tucked under Slick's arm.

"What the hell are you doing here? Are you trying to bury me?"

Now it was Slick's turn to smile. "I wouldn't pass up the opportunity."

Brandeal walked over to the captain. "Why is she here?"

"So I guess that means you two want to skip the tearful

reunion. Slick's agreed to look into your case," DeStasio explained. "You say you're innocent—"

"I am innocent," Brandeal said emphatically, interrupting him.

The captain ignored him and continued. "I wanted someone off the job to be on your side," DeStasio said.

"On my side? Her? Are you kidding me? Maybe when hell freezes over." Brandeal was outraged.

"Listen, Brandeal, Slick is a dedicated professional. She has earned the respect and confidence of the whole department statewide. She's got the reputation, the weight, and the profile liked by the bureaucracy, even with the courts. If she says you're innocent, no one will question it."

"I already don't like it. What if she says I'm guilty? She could manipulate the evidence against me, and no one would question that, either!" Brandeal yelled.

"Me planting evidence against you, Brandeal. Now, wouldn't that be a slice of irony pie," Slick said softly.

Brandeal backed up and angrily went to the captain's desk.

"Did you hear that, Captain? She's out to get me. I don't want her here. I don't need these two dykes."

"Watch it, Brandeal," Slick warned.

Brandeal turned back to Slick and looked angrily at her, then at Laura.

"Get the hell out. Both of you, Ebony and Ivory. Give my regards to Ellen, or whoever is the top lesbo this year, and let's chat when the new season of *The L-Word* starts."

"Your lips, my ass. They should meet."

Slick stepped back and really looked at him. His eyes were bloodshot, he needed a shave, and his clothes looked like they had been slept in.

"This murder is eating you up inside, isn't it, Brandeal? You're worried. You never were any good under pressure. And now you've got me to deal with. I just became your biggest problem. So if you have something to say, say it now."

"Oh, you ARE good! I'm just about to crack!"

Brandeal turned to DeStasio. "Please, Captain! Don't let her hurt me. Please make her stop!"

Brandeal laughed coldly and turned back to Slick. "Still big with the empty threats, I see. Get over yourself, Slick."

"Be very careful, Brandeal."

DeStasio tried to swallow his impatience with them before he spoke but was only minimally successful.

"I'm so glad you two took the course in witty banter at the academy. Now, can we act like adults?"

"She started it!"

"He started it!" Brandeal and Slick were pointing at each other.

"I wish you both could see yourselves at this moment," DeStasio sighed.

Slick and Brandeal ignored him.

"Can you account for your time, asshole? I want to know where you were that night. All of it. Chapter and verse," Slick demanded.

"Let me tell you everything you need to know, Homo-Cop. Pay attention. I'm only going to say this once—I didn't do it. I don't know who did. I had nothing to do with it. It wasn't me. Got that? It wasn't me. End of story. Now you're up to speed."

" 'It wasn't me.' That's original. Is that all you've got?"

Brandeal said nothing. He wasn't about to offer any explanations about his connection to a dead prostitute. Not to Slick. Never.

"You know what, Brandeal? I almost hope you did do it. You're in my world now, and if you killed that girl, I'm going to take you down. I promise you. I'm going to be all over you like weird on Michael Jackson."

"Oh, great. It'll be just me and my shadow." Then he added, "Bitch."

Brandeal never saw it coming. Slick punched him squarely in the face. "Eat fist, shithead."

Brandeal's eyes rolled back like someone about to lose consciousness. An expression of surprise briefly crossed his face, then vanished. His body hit the wall, and he slid limply to the floor, out cold. Then Slick stormed out of Captain DeStasio's office, slamming the door behind her.

# 12

Captain DeStasio and Laura sat looking at each other in the awkward quiet that followed. The only sound in the room was the ticking of the wall clock. The sound, which was barely audible before, was now sonorous and reverberated like a great gong being struck slowly.

Several long moments dragged by. Laura couldn't believe how uncomfortable her chair had suddenly become. She was certain it had been used to torture prisoners at Abu Ghraib.

"How long do you think we should sit here in stunned silence?" Laura asked finally in a wondering voice.

DeStasio was grateful that she had so graciously eased the tension in the room.

"I'd say that's long enough," he replied, smiling. He took a sip of his coffee. Then, stumbling to continue the conversation, he added, "I see Slick still has that sneaky left hook."

"Yes," Laura said, practically beaming. "It's part of her girlish charm."

"So, Captain, you put Slick and Mr. Brandeal back together again. How do you think it's going so far?" she asked.

Laura pronounced each syllable slowly so she could adjust her butt on the torture chair, inconspicuously she hoped.

"All things considered, I think it went well. I'm so optimistic, I'm preparing to do cartwheels." DeStasio's voice was heavy with sarcasm. He wasn't used to having his judgment questioned. He took another sip of his coffee.

"So you're taking that punch as a good sign?"

"No." It was time for the gambler to put some of his cards on the table. "I'm relying more on my hunch that Slick can't walk away from this case. If Brandeal did the murder, she'll have the satisfaction of knowing she was the one to get him. If he's innocent, she'll know it, because she worked the case herself. I know she has some personal issues with Brandeal. But that's the reason I trust her. She was too good a cop, too honest; if he's guilty, she'll explore every angle to be sure it isn't a personal vendetta."

Laura smiled because she understood him all at once. Captain DeStasio was a very good judge of human nature. "It was very nice meeting you, Captain. I'll be going now," she said. "I can't expect Slick to come back for me. That was too good an exit. Very dramatic. She's probably waiting for me downstairs."

Laura stood and picked up Garbo, who had been exuberantly sniffing and inspecting Brandeal's prostrate body. Her tail was still wagging with enthusiasm.

The captain started to rise from his seat as she was leaving.

"Please don't bother to get up, Captain," she said. Then, looking down at the still motionless Brandeal, she added, "And that goes double for you, Mr. Brandeal." Laura stepped daintily over him, slipped through the door, and was gone.

The captain was about to check on Brandeal when he heard the sounds of movement coming from the floor.

"What happened?" Brandeal asked slowly, massaging his jaw. He wondered momentarily why his face was wet, like it had been licked.

"How do you feel?" the captain asked.

"I feel like someone hit me in the face with a two-by-four."

"That's funny. Because Slick hit you in the face with a two-by-four."

"What? She hit me?"

"And knocked you out."

"That's only because she surprised me. You know I can take her."

"We'll never know."

"Oh, come on, Captain."

"Look at yourself. Your balls are all over the floor. You went down."

"But in a manly way, right? I went down swinging, right?"

"Don't flatter yourself, sissy boy. You went down faster than a pair of panties on prom night."

"But in a manly way, right?" Brandeal repeated, pressing now.

The captain said nothing. He moved some papers around on his desk and sipped his coffee.

"If word of this gets out . . ."

The captain shrugged and sighed. "Yeah. Sure, Brandeal. You were very manly. Very rugged. Whatever."

Brandeal was relieved. "Is Slick still your idea of a dedicated professional? She hit me."

"Well, she couldn't shoot you, could she? Not with all the witnesses in the room. You called her a bitch, so in her own way, she bitch-slapped you. Maybe you should close your mouth before you talk. You have a knack for cracking wise when you shouldn't. And if you're going to insult Slick, maybe you should be wearing a cup, just in case."

"I'll consider it."

DeStasio shifted his weight in his chair and cleared his throat. "I'm getting pretty tired of talking to you, Brandeal, so are there any other funny comments you'd like to make from your recumbent position before I send you back to your desk?"

There was a brief silence.

"You really need to get the ceiling painted." Brandeal coughed dryly. "Can I get some water down here?"

"How about a hot cup of shut the fuck up?"

"With cream. No sugar."

"You really want to piss me off, Brandeal? How 'bout I stick a broom up your ass and sweep the floor with you."

"You invited me to make a funny comment, Captain."

"I am not laughing, Brandeal. You should leave. Like now."

Brandeal knew he was testing the captain's patience, whose tone had gone from Condition Yellow to Condition Red. Brandeal worked himself up to his feet with an audible grunt and left.

The captain sat at his desk and watched the door close, glad to be alone to finish his coffee. Sometimes silence was life's greatest blessing.

# 13

"Bad day?"

Slick was so preoccupied with her anger at Tom Brandeal as she tore out of the captain's office that she hadn't heard the man now addressing her arrive at her side. She wheeled around sharply and looked into the kind eyes of her former partner.

"Sam," she said with affection. They exchanged a very brief hug, toned down to fit the surroundings.

Sam noticed she was shielding her left hand. "What happened to you?" he asked.

"It's nothing. Let's just say, yes, I'm having a bad day. I am having possibly the worst day of my whole life."

"DeStasio asked you to work the Tom Brandeal case, right?"

"How did you know?"

"Partner, we still have PNN."

Police News Network. Slick smiled. Everybody knew. There were very few secrets in a squad. Gossip traveled fast. Even the cockroaches were listening.

"You gonna do it?" Sam asked.

Before Slick could answer, Paula Rafferty and Cathy Simpson approached.

"Hey, what are you two doing here?" Slick asked, happy to see her old friends.

"We heard over the car radio that you were escorted back into the house," Cathy said. "We know Brandeal is in a jam, and we figured you were brought in to investigate. We had to stop by and pay our respects, show a little love."

"Damn, Slick, you lucky so-and-so." Paula was smiling and talking in a hushed conspiratorial tone. She playfully punched Slick on her left arm. No one noticed her wince in pain.

"You get to take down Tom Brandeal." She laughed. "Time for some poetic payback. We finally got him. Are angels singing or is it just me? It doesn't get much better than this." Then Paula put her hands together and rubbed them briskly and cheerfully, as if she had just sat down to a sumptuous feast.

"What do you mean?" Slick asked.

"Oh, come on, Slick," Paula whispered. "It's time for a little blue justice to be handed down. Time for Brandeal to get what's coming to him, and you're just the one to make sure he gets it."

Slick said nothing but looked very uncomfortable. Paula couldn't understand her lack of enthusiasm at having won the chance to exact some revenge on Tom Brandeal. She looked at Sam and Cathy for their reaction, trying to see if they understood what was going on with Slick. They both remained silent.

"Wait a minute, Slick," Paula continued, trying to make some sense of the situation. "I know you're not forgetting what Brandeal did to you on the Sean MacGuire case. That innocent man is dead because of him."

"You know I haven't forgotten that."

"And I know you remember how he treated all of us."

Slick just nodded and shifted her stance to put a little space between herself and Paula, but Paula didn't back down.

"But let's forget about all that for a minute. Brandeal didn't just piss off the blacks and gays here; he went over the line every time he could. He's not a credit to the job. He's no damn good, and he works at it full-time. No one wants to partner with him. No one's going to care if you make sure he's found guilty of this murder. He's ripe for it. Hell, some of us would celebrate his conviction."

"So by-the-book goes out the window?"

"When did Tom Brandeal ever play by the book? He blew the bindings off the book years ago."

"What if he's innocent?"

Paula couldn't believe what she was hearing from Slick and made no effort to mask her anger. "I don't get you, Slick. Sean MacGuire, he was innocent. Tom Brandeal has never spent an innocent day in his life, and you know it."

"Okay, but what about the family of Gloria Roxley. She's the one who was murdered. They may want to know who actually murdered her. Serving up Brandeal if he's innocent isn't going to give her family closure."

"It's a fact of life that sometimes family is collateral damage when you're going after something bigger."

"What would I tell them?"

"You wouldn't have to tell them anything. They wouldn't know the difference."

"I'd know."

"She was a prostitute, for Christ's sake. A prostitute that Brandeal was somehow involved with. There's more than one way to get a man guilty. You can make him dirty on this. He's done so much other shit, it will be easy. And, hey, if he really didn't do it, you can find a way to connect the dots from the murderer to Brandeal."

Slick tried hard to remain dispassionate, but deep down she understood Paula's rage. She had felt it herself for years while on the force.

Everyone knew that Slick had quit the force at Laura's insistence, because she feared for Slick's safety. Her cushy job of running Laura's clam company put an end to her day-to-day dealings with Brandeal, but her friends still had to roll around in the gutters and work with the son of a bitch.

She suddenly felt that by getting involved with Brandeal again, she was spreading dog shit on the bottom of her shoe and betraying her friends all at once. She was starting to wish she hadn't given her word to Captain DeStasio.

"Look, I don't like Brandeal any more than you do. I know he's a scumbag, but I can't—"

Paula wouldn't listen to any more. She got as close to Slick as she could. "Listen to yourself. You should be ashamed. I don't want to hear about what you *can't* do."

Cathy could see that Paula's words were affecting Slick. "Come on, Paula. Let's go," she said, trying to get Paula to calm down, but Paula didn't stop.

"Brandeal has crossed the last line. The trap is set and ready to spring. He deserves what's coming his way. So, if you *can't* do the right thing by making sure he's caught and taken down once and for all, you kick the case and let someone handle it who can. Step up or step off. You feel me?"

*Like I'm inside your skin,* Slick thought.

Paula turned away and walked quickly, wanting to put as much distance between herself and Slick as possible.

"Sorry, Slick," Cathy said. "You do what you gotta do. I'll try to reason with her." Then Cathy took off after her partner.

Slick watched her go. It had been a sincere apology, Slick thought, but she was certain she had seen that same look of disappointment on Cathy's face, too.

Slick couldn't recall ever having had a disagreement with either of them. She wondered if they would ever get back to their old friendship.

Then, as she self-consciously turned around to face Sam, she saw the stares of other officers who were standing nearby and who had probably heard her confrontation with Paula. They stared at her for a moment, then went back to what they were doing.

Sam said nothing as he stood alone with his old partner. He would support her no matter how she did the investigation, but he knew there would only be one way Slick would do it. He knew Paula's words hurt her, and he knew she'd speak when she was ready, so he said nothing.

"Well, one good thing is," Slick said, sighing, trying to cheer herself up, "whatever happens, at least now the Internal Affairs Bureau is on to Brandeal. They'll catch up with him and find some of the shit he's been up to."

Sam said nothing.

Slick could see in his face something was wrong. "Sam?"

Sam looked at the floor and took a deep breath. Then he looked Slick squarely in the eyes. "The captain never contacted IAB about Brandeal."

Slick was in disbelief. "He just told me did. He said that Brandeal was restricted to a desk job."

"That much is true. Brandeal has been pulled inside. But IAB has not been contacted about this."

"Are you sure?"

"Yeah, I checked it out. I have contacts at IAB."

"Why would DeStasio tell me he contacted them if he didn't?"

Again Sam was silent.

Slick shook her head as if trying to clear it. "Let's see if I've got this straight. I'm working a murder case to help clear a man I hate, which has led to the worst argument I've ever had with one of my best friends, and my former captain, a man I respect, isn't being totally honest with me?"

"That about sums it up," Sam said.

Slick looked despondent.

"I guess it could be worse," Sam added.

"It is worse, Sam," she said softly.

"How?"

Slick just sighed wearily and said nothing. She saw Laura coming down the stairs.

"Hopefully," she said, "I'll wake up tomorrow, find Patrick Duffy standing in my shower, and this whole nightmare will be over."

# 14

Laura, with Garbo tucked under her arm, found Slick standing with Sam downstairs from DeStasio's office. They both seemed to brighten up when they saw her approach.

Laura kissed Sam's cheek. "Hello, Sam," she said, smiling. "Good to see you."

"You too, Laura."

"So, what are you going to do now?" Sam asked Slick.

"I guess we'll go pay Cutter a visit."

Then they both laughed like they were sharing a private joke.

"Who's Cutter?" Laura asked, wanting in on the joke.

"Cutter Meldrick is the medical examiner," Sam explained. "And he's a little out there."

"Out as in gay and out?" Laura asked.

"No, out as in far out. Off the grid. Outer-space out. When E.T. phoned home, I think Cutter was the one who answered the call."

Laura looked at him, not understanding.

Sam laughed. "I can't describe Cutter. You'll have to experience him for yourself." Then Sam winked at Slick and reached for Garbo.

"You better leave her with me. They'd never let her in the building."

Sam scooped her up then buried his face in her fur. Garbo nuzzled him with her cold wet nose, tickling him.

As Slick and Laura walked away, Sam said, "I'm here for you, partner. Anything you need. Anything. I'm on it."

"Thanks, Sam."

Sam watched as Slick and Laura walked away and left the building.

He looked over at Paula and saw that Cathy was still trying to calm her down. It didn't appear to be working. Eventually, Cathy gave up, walked away, and went back to her desk.

Sam walked over to his desk, put Garbo on his chair and pulled out the chew toy from a drawer he kept there for her visits. When he was sure she was settled in, he walked over to Paula.

He stood at her desk for a few moments, neither of them speaking.

Finally Paula lifted her head and looked at him with an attitude. "Listen, Sam," she said. "I don't need a lecture from you. I just got one from Cathy."

"I'm not going to lecture you."

"Then what do you want?"

"You know, Slick's gonna need our help on this."

"You saw me; I tried. She doesn't seem to want my help."

"From where I was standing, you weren't offering her help. You were just trying to get her to pin this whole thing on Brandeal. That's not how Slick works."

"Why not? This time he's probably guilty."

"You can help by letting her do her investigation without interference and without judging her. It's just possible Brandeal could be innocent of this murder."

"Yeah, sure. Do you really believe that?"

Sam sighed and looked away. He had worked with Paula too long. He knew he couldn't bullshit her. Even now when he wasn't looking directly at her, he could feel her solemn brown eyes scanning his face for his reaction.

"That's what I thought," Paula said.

"It doesn't matter what I think about Brandeal. Slick has always done things by the book. She's not about to change now."

Paula turned away and started to go through some of the paperwork on her desk. "Hey, what the hell do I care anyway," she said casually. "This has got nothing to do with me. Why should I waste my time going over old shit? I've got my own cases to solve. This is Slick's problem."

"Then you'll give Slick all the support she needs?"

"Absolutely."

Sam said nothing.

"Anything else?" Paula asked.

"No."

"Well, then, can I get back to my work now?"

Sam nodded, not believing a word she said. Paula couldn't bullshit him, either.

He went back to his desk.

Paula felt the old anger burning in her veins. She could not ignore it. She would make sure Brandeal got what was coming to him.

# 15

The regional medical examiner's office in Newark was two blocks from the Newark Police Department. It serviced Passaic, Essex, Hudson, and Somerset counties, handling about twelve hundred autopsies a year.

The two-story redbrick-and-concrete complex was complete with seven toxicology labs, autopsy rooms, libraries, conference rooms, offices, and two morgues.

Slick and Laura entered the facility and were immediately struck by the vague odor of alcohol and room deodorizer. The walls and floors were spotless and gleaming.

After identifying themselves and signing in at the security desk, they proceeded to the office of Dr. Meldrick. The door to his office was open, but no one was inside.

On the wall opposite Dr. Meldrick's desk was a series of monitors that televised and recorded the proceedings in the autopsy rooms.

Slick and Laura stepped inside the office, drawn to what appeared on the monitors. Several autopsies were in progress. Corpses and body parts were visible on all the screens. Neither wanted to look, but neither could look away.

In the various rooms MEs were moving surgical carts, operating autopsy saws, dissecting organs on cutting boards, and washing unrecognizable items in sinks. From time to time, an ME would disappear into a walk-in refrigerator.

Then, on one of the screens, they watched as a stainless-steel cadaver carrier with a body in a pouch was pushed into view. The unseen examiner switched on a magnifying lamp and positioned it close to the corpse's head.

Slick and Laura were riveted to the screen, giving in to ghoulish curiosity.

The body pouch was carefully unzipped and spread open. The victim had red hair that was damp and still gory with bits of brain and other tissue. One eye was missing as well as several teeth. The head was almost totally severed.

There was almost nothing left of the face, almost nothing left of the skull. It looked as if a small explosion blew everything away. They couldn't tell if the dead body was a man or a woman.

"Suicide."

Surprised, Slick and Laura spun around and were greeted by the gap-toothed grin of Dr. Meldrick.

"Still sneaking up on people, Cutter? That never gets old." Slick hoped her voice didn't reveal just how much he had startled her. She had forgotten how Meldrick loved to play his little jokes.

"Shotgun blast into the mouth. Not very pretty, is it?" Meldrick continued, studying the screen, thoroughly satisfied that he had successfully spooked the former detective.

"Used her big toe to pull the trigger. Now that shows a real determination, an unwavering commitment, if you will, to get the job done right," he said. "No trifling with unreliable pills or poisons for this one. Oh, no. Just the faultless precision of a shotgun blast in the mouth. One click, then *POW!* Gray matter splattered on the wallpaper."

"Please seek therapy soon, Cutter," Slick said stiffly.

Meldrick smiled and dismissed her with a wave of his hand, then turned his full attention to Laura.

"That's *Carter*, Ms. Charles. Dr. Carter Meldrick," he said, introducing himself to Laura and taking a step closer to her, trying to experience every bit of her.

"The nickname Cutter is an obvious and crude reference to my job." When he shook her hand, he was glad to see she wasn't wearing a wedding ring. He was completely enthralled by Laura and couldn't take his eyes off her.

Laura immediately understood what Sam had said about the medical examiner. Dr. Carter Meldrick stood over six feet tall with an unmistakable munchkinlike nasal whine, equal parts Truman Capote and Pee-wee Herman.

His cockeyed left eye seemed to wander off on its own. Under his extra-long flowing lab coat, he was wearing a T-shirt that read I SEE DEAD PEOPLE. He looked like a long-lost relative of the Addams Family.

Laura correctly assumed that Dr. Carter Meldrick, chief medical examiner, was a man at peace with his morbid life's work, and even after the years of the atrocities he had seen, he maintained a sense of humor about the dark absurdities of life and death.

"Captain DeStasio called and said you and Ms. Charles might be paying me a visit, Detective. How can I help you?" His eyes never left Laura.

"You did the autopsy report on a Gloria Roxley," Slick answered. "May I see it?"

"Certainly. My autopsy report is your autopsy report." He was grinning at Laura.

Laura smiled back at him. She didn't find his staring lascivious or leering. It was merely sheepish and goofy.

Meldrick waved the Gloria Roxley report in Slick's general direction, barely acknowledging that she was even in the room.

"You need to get out more often, Meldrick," Slick said, noticing the effect Laura was having on him. "Still living with your mother?"

Meldrick ignored her. "I'm sorry for staring, Ms. Charles," Meldrick said sincerely. "I'm not currently seeing anyone. It's difficult, you know. I don't get to meet a lot of beautiful single women doing this job. Of course, I meet plenty of new widows here, yes, but asking them out on a date? I don't know. The timing just seems, well, wrong. Know what I mean?"

Laura tried to speak, but before she could, Meldrick took a deep breath and continued. "I know this is forward, Ms. Charles, but no one appreciates the term *carpe diem* better than a medical examiner. I've learned you've got to jump in and suck the marrow of life. Would you possibly consider having dinner—"

"I'm very flattered, Dr. Meldrick," Laura interrupted, "but I'm not single."

Meldrick's gaze went from Laura to Slick, then back again several times.

Slick thought he looked like an owl clock gone berserk.

Then Meldrick understood. "I'm so very sorry," he said. "Of course, I knew that Detective Slick was . . . but I didn't know . . . Please forgive me." Meldrick's face was almost purple with embarrassment.

"Forget it, Meldrick," Slick said. She was looking through the file. "Your toxicology report doesn't show the presence of any alcohol or drugs in her system."

"That's because there were no toxins present."

"That's strange."

"Why?"

"The witnesses at the motel said that Gloria appeared to be intoxicated that night. Very intoxicated. And the witness saw her shortly before she was killed."

"There's absolutely no medical evidence to support that. She was clean."

Slick continued thoughtfully. "And you list the cause of her death to be a broken neck. There was so much blood at the crime scene and on the hotel bedding she was wrapped in when she was found in the car trunk that I just assumed she died from the multiple stab wounds and that somehow her neck was broken afterward."

"No. The other way around. Her neck was broken before she died. That's what killed her. The stab wounds were inflicted postmortem, almost as an afterthought. I can show you if you like. She's right back there, a guest in the fridge motel."

Laura's stomach lurched, and her eyes went wide. She had had enough of the autopsies on the monitors. She was sure the terrible images would pop up in her dreams for weeks to come. She wasn't sure she could keep it together if she saw an autopsy up close and personal. She hoped Slick would pass on viewing Gloria Roxley's corpse.

Slick was silent, considering Meldrick's invitation. "No. I don't think that will be necessary. You're crazy, but you're the best. I'll take your word for it," she said finally, trying to recover the ability to speak. Her voice was a long time coming, as if it had been trapped in her throat. She almost didn't get the words out. Her mouth was dry, and dryness made her tongue clumsy.

Maybe Slick had sensed Laura's reluctance to view the body, or maybe the strain of the day was catching up with her. Laura wasn't sure, she was just grateful not to have to view an autopsied corpse in painstaking detail.

Dr. Meldrick looked at his watch.

"Well, then, Detective, if there's nothing more I can do for you, I'll get back to my beautiful bodies and leave you with a case to solve."

"Beautiful?" Slick blurted out.

"Yes, beautiful!"

Meldrick laughed softly at their horrified expressions. "Well, I suppose I see corpses differently than most people. Remember that for every surgical procedure developed, from heart transplants to gender reassignment surgery, cadavers have been there, alongside the surgeons making history."

"In their own quiet way," Slick joked.

"That's right," Meldrick continued, as if he had missed the joke. "Ask yourself this—where would we be without corpses? They've added to the betterment of mankind. From the very beginning, they were there for testing surgical incisions and training young doctors in medical school classrooms. They have helped make the case for mandatory seat belts and have ridden in the space shuttle."

Meldrick had Slick and Laura enthralled.

"They are superheroes, really, when you think about it," Meldrick continued. "They can be dismembered, cut open, and rearranged. They can be in six places at once. You can burn them, throw them off buildings, place them into head-on crashes."

He didn't notice that Slick and Laura exchanged a squeamish look.

"Why, you can fire a gun at them, run a speedboat over their legs, and even take their heads off and they remain unfazed."

"Okay, Meldrick, that's enough. We get it," Slick said.

Perhaps he had lost them again, he thought. "Certainly," he said. "Just trying to provide a new perspective on the dead."

"We felt it," Laura tried to assure him, feeling a little sorry for him.

Meldrick was about to walk away, when he turned around and added, "Lovely mystery, isn't it? Gloria Roxley's death. No alcohol, no drugs in an apparently intoxicated woman, and massive amounts of blood that the injuries couldn't produce. Most contradictory. Baffling! God, I love this stuff." He was undeniably exhilarated by it all.

Meldrick took Laura's hand and kissed it. He held on to it a moment, cradling it gently in his hands, running his fingers along her skin, savoring the softness, memorizing it. It wasn't often that he got to touch living flesh. "Thanks for bringing a little sunshine in here, Ms. Charles," he said, and was out the door as quickly and silently as he had entered, leaving Slick and Laura to wonder what body part he'd be touching next.

# 16

Twilight was approaching, and Slick's hand hurt more intensely now from punching Brandeal, even after soaking it in ice repeatedly since leaving the medical examiner's office. Laura sat beside her and helped her ease into an Ace bandage.

Slick hadn't spoken much since coming home. She had drifted deeply into her own faraway thoughts.

"Scorsese called," Laura said sprightly, making sure the Ace bandage wasn't too tight. "He wants you for the lead in his new fight film *Raging Bull Dyke*."

Slick had to laugh in spite of her pain. The sound of her laughter made her aware that she hadn't said a word in hours. "Have I apologized enough for storming out and leaving you? I can't believe I lost it like that, right in the captain's office. Not exactly the picture of grace under pressure, was I?" Her tone was hushed and ashamed.

"You don't have to apologize to me," Laura assured her. "I saw how Mr. Brandeal provoked you. It's obvious you two will never exchange valentines."

Laura tried to keep Slick talking now. "You've been very

quiet. Are you having second thoughts about accepting the case?"

"No. DeStasio was my captain, and he is a fair and honest man."

However, there was the IAB issue, but Slick didn't want to deal with that yet. DeStasio must have had his reasons for not being totally forthcoming about it. She decided to give him the benefit of the doubt for now.

"I would do whatever I could for him. As for Brandeal, the guy's an idiot, always has been. He got away with some pretty sleazy stuff on the job. I'd never figure him for a murderer, though."

"And now?"

"I don't know," Slick sighed. "What makes a dirty cop cross that final line? Why didn't he have Paradise registered as a confidential informant? Why didn't he want a paper trail on her?" Slick tried to flex her hand before she continued. "And did you see the way he looked? Very unkempt and he smelled like he's been living off cigarettes and scotch. Could be that he's innocent and just reacting badly to being under suspicion of a murder and being assigned to a desk job until this is all cleared up, or it could be something worse."

"But what else is going on?" Laura asked. "What else is bothering you?"

"Nothing's bothering me." Damn, Slick thought. She had answered too quickly and too casually.

Laura just looked at her, studying her face, trying to read the information she was withholding.

"You're lying, aren't you?"

Slick looked into her blue eyes. *It's useless,* she thought, then sighed and gave in. "Through my teeth," Slick admitted.

"Then I can wait."

Laura crossed her arms over her chest and crossed her legs and became immovable. She meant business.

Slick knew the pose.

Laura would "wait" for all of ten seconds—her waiting threshold when she felt Slick had brooded long enough; then she would start grilling her with questions.

"If I have to, I can sit here until I grow roots," Laura said. That was the signal that the ten seconds was almost up.

Slick looked out the bedroom window at the vivid streaks of blue and red searing the evening sky. The sun was making a brilliant last stand before slipping below the hills, making way for the approaching cover of night.

It had been hours now. One of the worst days of her life was coming to an end. Keeping everything pent up inside wasn't working. It never did. When would she learn that? If she didn't start talking now, the specter from her past would linger with her until morning.

"What's bothering me is the prostitute Paradise. Gloria Roxley. I was in love with her."

That revelation jolted Laura out of her pose, like a shock of electricity had passed through her body. A million things came into her head, but she didn't give voice to any of them. Now that Slick was talking, it was best to hear her out.

Slick continued. "We were twelve years old at the time. We went to school together in Newark. Gloria was the first girl I ever had a crush on. The first girl I ever kissed. That one kiss explained everything for me. It all fell into place after that. I knew I was gay."

Slick paused, remembering the moment, remembering the kiss and the powerful realization that came with it. The memory moved like a warm light through her soul.

"Sadly, for me," she said, laughing slightly, "Gloria realized she wasn't gay, but we still cared about each other. She was my best friend. She accepted me unconditionally. She never made me feel like a freak. I made her promise not to tell anyone I was gay. I even came up with some silly ceremony where we pricked our fingers, drew blood, and pressed them together in a blood oath. 'Promise not to tell.' We took those words as seriously as if they had been finalized by a team of lawyers. Whenever one of us said it, the other knew we were about to hear a secret that we'd have to take to the grave.

"Gloria kept her promise to me. She never said a word to anyone. She let me come out when I was ready and on my own terms, knowing that no matter what, she would always be my friend.

"When you're a kid, you take for granted that the people you grow up with will always be there. After that, we made other childhood promises to stay in touch. You know, the kinds of stuff you write in your friends' high school yearbooks. But, well, you know how that goes. Her family moved away, and she went to another school.

"Years later, I heard that she had become a pross. I couldn't believe it. I wanted to get in touch with her, find out what the hell happened, but I never did. Every time I tried to reach out to her, she'd never get back to me. Finally I stopped trying. I haven't thought about her in a long time."

Laura saw pain on her face.

"And now she's been murdered. If Tom Brandeal killed her, if he turned her into some DOA dump job . . . I can't let this be my last memory of her. I couldn't stand it. . . ."

Slick's voice faded. It was a few moments before she spoke again.

"Gloria's the reason I took the case. I think I owe her that much," she said softly.

After that there was another small silence.

Laura lifted Slick's cast-down face. "Then we'll find out what happened to Gloria. She helped you find yourself. For that, I think I owe her something, too." She kissed Slick's eyelids.

Slick would remember the feel of Laura's soft touch and her kindness at this moment forever. Slick just looked at her and smiled. It was from her heart and it spoke volumes.

"I love you, too," Laura said.

"I didn't say a word."

"And yet I heard you," Laura purred in Slick's ear.

Slick gave Laura a hug, then she lifted her hand and said, "Up here."

They did a high five, realizing too late that Slick had used her injured hand.

"Ouch!" she said through her laughter.

"Are you in a lot of pain?"

"Well, I won't be sparring with Laila Ali any time soon, but I could go a few rounds with you."

Slick pulled Laura close and kissed her. Her lips were soft and moist. "I'm not sure you can handle me. I'm in the mood for a lot of bobbing and weaving," Laura teased. She started unbuttoning Slick's shirt and kissed her deeply, invitingly.

"Was that a challenge kiss?"

"No. This is a challenge kiss." This time the kiss was demanding.

"Then I accept your challenge and promise you a hell of a bout."

"Are you really sure you can take me on? I'm not going to pull any punches."

"Bring it, bruiser. No holds barred. Hit me with your best shot. You're just a featherweight, and I know I can lick you with one hand tied behind my back."

Laura's laughter was low and lusty. "I bet you could."

"Oh, this is so on," Slick said.

They put their arms around each other and playfully tumbled back onto the bed only to bounce back up almost instantly when they realized Garbo was under them.

"Garbo, go to your bed," they said in unison.

The dog didn't move. Her pet bed on the floor was comfortable, but she preferred to sleep on the big bed with them.

Slick pointed to the dog bed with fake anger and said, "I hear cats make good pets."

Garbo quickly jumped down and obediently went to her own bed. There she turned around twice, then sat down. She perked up her ears and listened, then sighed, resting her head on her front paws and closing her eyes, resigned to her fate.

She knew from the sounds coming from the big bed that she'd be spending the whole night alone on the floor.

# 17

DeStasio looked at the photograph of his wife that was taken on their wedding day. That photo had been placed prominently on every desk he'd ever had. Now that she was gone, he looked at it and felt like she was watching over him. He wondered if she would have approved of his actions today.

What he hadn't told Slick was that he had not reported Brandeal to Internal Affairs.

In the years since Slick had left the job, the IAB had become a joke. The cops who were supposed to police other cops did a lousy job of investigating. Some of the police assigned to the bureau were under criminal investigation themselves. The attorney general's office was currently doing a review of the bureau. Rumors were circulating that complaints of police brutality, theft, and other serious crimes had never even been entered into the system.

Red flags were going up, signaling that after the probe was completed, the shake-up would be bad, and IAB would come back harder, looking to prosecute even the slightest infraction of the rules to regain public trust.

Captain DeStasio didn't want to risk putting Brandeal

into that mess now. He didn't know if Brandeal was innocent or not, but his years as captain made him loyal to his officers. If Brandeal was a murderer, though, the captain knew he would go down with him for failing to report him. At least those were the reasons he gave himself to justify why he hadn't called IAB. They were true enough. IAB was a total disaster, but there were other reasons. Reasons far more personal to the captain for keeping a close rein on Brandeal's activities. He wasn't prepared to share those private reasons with Slick just yet. He looked again at the picture of his wife. He could almost feel her disapproval. DeStasio was risking a lot.

The captain's chips were all in; he was rolling the dice big-time, and the game was just getting started.

# 18

The bartender on duty at McMurphy's Tavern looked around the dark and dismal room, through the clouds of rank tobacco smoke that hung in the air, and knew that the drunk at the end of the bar was going to be trouble.

It was almost closing time, and the bartender could always tell the ones he'd have to get physical with to get them out the door. Knowing this required no great amount of psychic ability. When you'd been a bartender as long as he had, you got so you could spot the ones looking to get bounced; you could spot them a mile away.

A sure sign was when the guy never reached into the complimentary dish of peanuts placed in front of him. Another was when the guy never looked up at the semi-nude dancers.

The girls worked the bar top, stopping to dance for each man seated at the bar for about fifteen seconds before moving on to the next man. This guy didn't look up for a single grind or even a "crack shot" as the girls liked to call it. When a man didn't notice that a woman was undulating her crotch in his face, something was definitely wrong.

This particular souse had been drinking nonstop since he came in, pausing only long enough to get up to relieve himself.

On those woozy staggerings into the men's room, he would sway and stumble into other drinkers at the bar who hadn't quite crawled into their bottles as far as he had.

Meaningless curses and impotent threats were exchanged when he blundered into his fellow travelers, only to be forgotten until he had to get up again to take another piss.

"Splash some more scotch against these rocks," the drunk would say when he was ready for a refill.

About five refills ago, the scotch had started to slop out of the glass as he raised it to his lips. He attacked each new drink with dangerous gusto, like he was trying to drown himself with fire instead of water.

The girls had quit dancing over half an hour ago, the crowd had thinned, and the last of the regular idlers straggled out one by one when the bartender called, "Closing time" and flashed the lights, but just as he had suspected, the drunk at the end of the bar didn't budge.

The bartender turned off the outside neon McMURPHY'S sign and watched the drunk until there was no one else left in the bar.

"Okay, buddy, time to go," he said loudly.

The drunk didn't move.

"Hey, you! It's closing time. Let's go."

The drunk simply looked at him and let out a long disgusting belch. Then he smirked at the bartender.

*Okay, time to break bad,* the bartender thought. He stole a quick glance at the nail-studded baseball bat he had hidden under the counter but didn't think the situation called for that just yet. Instead, the bartender reasoned, this was where his workouts at the gym would pay off.

The drunken smart-ass didn't know who he was dealing with.

The bartender was feeling pumped now. His ego reared itself. Maybe he would slug this jerk and even knock out a tooth or two.

He assumed his most menacing scowl, then went flying at the drunk at the end of the bar, got in his face, and tried to intimidate him with sheer brawn. Still, the drunk remained motionless and unflinching.

Time for plan B. The bartender grabbed hold of the drunk's jacket collar and hauled him up from the bar stool. "Listen, pal," he said. "I don't want to hurt you. Don't make me call the cops."

The drunk pulled out his badge. "I am a cop, dickhead, and I am having a helluva bad day, understand? I am not in a mood that is particularly good. So, if you don't want me to close this crummy dive down for serving booze to underage drinkers, you'll take your fucking hands off me and back away—and quick, because I am the excitable type."

His words were slurred and his eyes were unfocused, but the bartender didn't challenge him. Instead, he gingerly guided the drunk cop back onto the bar stool and released his jacket collar.

"Very good, dickhead. Now, scurry away quickly. I'll let you know when it's time to close."

"Yes, sir. I'll just go close out the register." The bartender, proven ineffectual and feeling deflated, smiled nervously and walked away quickly as instructed.

Tom Brandeal lifted his drink and wondered why everything was still so clear to him. He was drunk, but everything that happened was still clear. Painfully clear. He had planned it so simply. Every detail, simple. Only simple murders succeed.

Brandeal suddenly remembered every time in his long career that he had cavalierly stepped over the line of ethical conduct without remorse and had never gotten caught.

Had he become so arrogant that he assumed he could really get away with the perfect murder?

And now Slick was working the case. Goddammit. He had dug himself into a pit, and she would be the one to throw the dirt in over him. He snorted contemptuously.

Brandeal wondered just how long he could last in prison with convicts who were there because of evidence he had massaged to put them there. They would see it as payback time. He thought he had braced for this, but now the full impact of that very real possibility hit him.

He rubbed his temples, but it didn't stop the noise. Brandeal was sure that the noise ringing in his head was the sardonic laughter of Fate as it cocked the big cosmic you-are-so-fucked gun at him. The laughter was only getting louder. He heard the laughter even when he wasn't drunk. It rasped against his skull like a dentist's drill.

He shook his head and tried to concentrate only on the glass in front of him, fingering the edge of it, trying to focus only on the glass, because if he thought about his part in the murder of Gloria Roxley anymore tonight, he was sure he'd go mad.

He was tired of thinking and needed rest. But if he went home now and tried to sleep, it would just be hours of tossing and turning before he had to report for work. He held his head in his hands momentarily as if to keep it from flying apart.

Then Brandeal sat up straight and tossed back the last of his drink.

"Hey, dickhead," he called out to the bartender. "Splash some more scotch against these rocks."

## This Is Action News 10 in New Jersey . . . All of New Jersey All of the Time

"Good morning. I'm Michelle Tevotino. With only days left until the election, it seems that Republican Pete Moreno got a boost in his ratings. Several polls say that Moreno won the debate, scoring a major victory over Democrat Clinton Kendall. What seemed to be a lead for Kendall has evaporated. Latest polls show the two men in a virtual dead heat. With four percent of the likely voters still undecided, *The Trentonian* has come out and endorsed Moreno.

"And in the Kim Shaw case, the jury stayed out for six hours. Then they brought in a guilty verdict. In a press conference just moments ago, the foreman said that Prosecutor Hamilton Baker proved beyond a reasonable doubt that Kim Shaw was guilty of murder."

# 19

There was a timid knock at his office door. That wasn't a good sign, the man inside thought. Now what?

"Come in," he said, the annoyance in his voice obvious.

The visitor stepped in and immediately avoided his eyes, feeling more comfortable looking at the floor.

The man got up from his desk and went to his bar.

"I was just about to make myself a gin and tonic. Will you join me, or is it too early for you?"

"Never too early for me. If you're pouring, I'm drinking."

They sat for a few moments in silence. The only sound in the room was the ice tinkling in their gin and tonics.

Finally he spoke. "I'm guessing this is not a social call."

"No, I'm afraid it's not. I got some bad news." The visitor shifted nervously in his chair.

"Go on. I'm listening." His voice was tight.

The visitor cleared his throat before continuing. "We've got a problem. The diary wasn't at her house. I checked like you wanted just to be sure. She must have mailed it like she said."

"Well," he said, sighing, "I'm very disappointed. I fear I may have been wrong about you."

"I know this is a screwup. If I could kick my own ass, I would." He smiled, trying to gain some mileage out of what he thought was a humorous remark.

His host wasn't smiling back at him. "I thought you could handle this assignment."

"I can."

"You've botched this job from the very beginning."

"This is just a little setback."

"A little setback? You assured me you would get the diary from the girl. You didn't. I was forced to dispose of her."

The visitor cringed at the memory.

The man noticed the fear in his visitor's eyes. He liked that. He took a long sip from his drink, giving his visitor more time to relive the memory.

"How are you going to gain entrance into the Owen Charles Foundation?"

"I know someone close to Laura Charles. I can talk to her."

"Don't disappoint me again."

There was a sharp edge to his tone, as rough as ragged glass. The way his hand stiffened around his gin and tonic, the visitor thought he would crush the glass into shards.

"I won't." He tried his best to sound convincing.

"Who is this friend?"

"An old friend she went to school with. It's a long story. Just give me some time to get it."

"I'm not happy. I don't like this at all. You do whatever you have to do, you understand?"

"Yes."

"That diary can seriously affect all my plans."

"I understand."

"I can't afford any more mistakes."

"I know that."

"Let me be perfectly clear here. Let me be emphatic. *You* can't afford to make any more mistakes." Then the man grinned. There was something feverish and unnatural about it.

"I know. I'll handle it." His throat was suddenly dry. He gulped down the rest of his gin and tonic.

"You'd better," he said. "You only have one more chance to get this right."

"I won't mess this up."

"I hope not."

The phone began to ring.

"Please show yourself out. I have other business to attend to."

The visitor did as he was told. He almost tripped over his own feet hurrying out the door.

As soon as the door closed, the man picked up the phone. His entire demeanor changed.

"Yes, I'm on my way, " he said cheerfully. There was an upcoming press conference he had to prepare for. He hung up, his mood becoming dark again as his thoughts returned to the diary and how bad it would be if it fell into the wrong hands.

# 20

Devlyn O'Hare couldn't believe her eyes or her luck. Here was her golden opportunity.

She held in her hands a little diary that contained the names of some of New Jersey's and New York's business, professional, and political royalty. She didn't have to look or fight for it. She didn't have to do anything devious to get it. It just came to her in the morning mail, along with all the other nondescript pieces of mail, the utility bills, the funding requests, the thank-yous for money given.

It just fell out of the envelope into her waiting hands, because it was bulkier and therefore more noticeable than the other mail. It was as though it had been mailed to her directly.

Well, actually it had been mailed to Laura, but with Laura spending more time working with Slick, it was decided that Devlyn would open any and all correspondence sent to the foundation.

Inside, next to the names of the social elite, were descriptions of their sexual preferences and pleasures. Devlyn turned every page with frenzied hands, eagerly soaking up the detailed images of upper-class perversity.

Devlyn couldn't be sure, but for the first time in her life, she thought she was blushing. Could this thing be real? Who sent it? And why was it sent to Laura at her charity? A surge of excitement coursed through her. She felt herself getting wet. If the writings contained in this journal were true, oh, the things she could demand from these powerful people with this kind of information.

She ran her fingers gingerly along the width of it. The very feel of it and the power that seemed to emanate from its pages thrilled her.

"Pinch me," she whispered hoarsely. The giddiness she felt was a challenge to her self-control. She gave in to her joy and allowed herself a one-footed twirl in her expensive leather chair. Then Devlyn let her attention drift outside the window. Focused now, she looked at the city beyond with the eyes of a bird of prey.

She was trying to visualize the big picture. Hell, with this kind of power, she could paint the big picture and control the city she gazed upon.

This book gave her the keys to the city.

Outside, the sun was continuing to rise, and she could feel her own star starting to rise as well. When it did, she'd be known as something other than Laura Charles's assistant.

Devlyn wanted things. She wanted things she didn't even know she wanted yet. She'd have her own respected position, her own power. More powerful than Laura. Devlyn didn't think that was too much to ask. Maybe then Laura would see her differently.

If the information she had in her possession was true, the destruction she could wreak could be biblical.

She brought her gaze back from the far horizon and concentrated on the book in her hands. She needed time to think. Opening her office door, she barked an order to her secretary that she was not available for anyone, to hold all her calls. She slammed the door, locked it, then hurried to the windows and drew the blinds, carefully, spying from behind them to make sure no one was watching her. You never knew whose telephoto lens might be looking in.

She went back to her desk and sat down in rigid concentration, head erect, delicate nostrils extended, eyes alert and focused.

What to do? Where to begin? Her mind raced through the possibilities. She got up from the desk and started a steady march back and forth across her carpeted office floor. Her movement was graceful and agile, like a jungle animal; she paused every now and then to throw anxious, furtive glances at her desk to make sure the diary was still there.

Outside her window, Devlyn noticed a small airplane towing a thirty-by-one-hundred-foot flying billboard. When the plane turned, Devlyn could read the advertisement.

VOTE FOR CLINTON KENDALL
FOR UNITED STATES SENATOR
"KENDALL CARES ABOUT NEW JERSEY"

On her drive in to the office, Devlyn remembered all the signs she saw along the way without paying much attention.

A VOTE FOR PETE MORENO
IS A VOTE FOR FAMILY VALUES & LOWER TAXES
"I NEED YOUR HELP"

Then she became inspired. Of course. She knew what she had to do. Her face lit up, and a sly smile, filled with self-appreciation, parted her soft moist lips.

Devlyn picked up the phone and made what she thought would be the most consequential call she'd ever make. She knew the most valuable of all commodities was information. Good information came with a price tag, and she knew the man she was calling would agree. She was certain he would give her what she wanted for this inside information.

Devlyn was nervous, but by the time the connection was made and the important man  was on the line, her voice was cool, calm, and clear, almost flirtatious. She crossed her legs and sat back, made herself comfortable in the leather chair. Now she was ready to play the game. Hell, she invented the game.

And as she coyly explained what she had in her possession, and how this would affect the interests of the man listening, she could almost feel the accoutrements of power being laid at her feet.

# 21

Slick and Laura spent hours talking to the Halsey Street regulars trying to gather information on Paradise. Just about everyone had seen her that night, and many knew that she worked as a snitch for Tom Brandeal, but no one could say with certainty that the man she was talking with the night she died was in fact Brandeal.

The subject was on everyone's lips. The crowd spoke about it in hushed subdued tones.

After three hours of interviews, there still were no good leads.

"When one is temporarily stalled on a homicide investigation, one must revivify with a quick libation," Slick said.

"Are you quoting directly from the police manual?" Laura asked

"In fact, I am. Page six. You thirsty?"

"Parched."

"Me, too. I think we need a trip to the Whip. I'm suffering from a martini deficiency."

"With extra olives for nutritional value."

The new and improved Kitten with a Whip women's bar

was a far cry from the dingy little hole-in-the-wall it had been twenty years ago. Then, lesbians came to swill beer, shoot a little pool, and maybe dance with another woman to tunes playing on an old jukebox. It was a casual welcoming hangout, so small and discreet that most passersby never gave it a second look. It was a place where women felt free to assume the butch or fem roles that they couldn't show out in the straight world.

Now, with its bilevel lesbian bar and restaurant with a dance club, it glowed like a beacon. The place had two crackling fireplaces, plasma TVs, and an adult store on a lower level. On any night of the week, there was a wide variety of young women cruising and flirting in the subtle lighting and to not-so-subtle music. They gathered here to discuss women's issues over dinner, mingle, and dance. The times had changed, but the need to be among other lesbians had not.

They started walking toward the bar.

"Stop where you are and put your hands in the air."

They did as they were told.

"You have the right to remain . . . fabulous."

When Slick and Laura turned around, they saw Lady Dijonnaise and Sheleeta Buffet pretending to point guns at them.

"We seen you out here canvassing the sex providers. Did you get anything you could use?" Lady asked.

Slick shook her head with deliberation. "Everyone saw her, but no one saw the man she was with," Slick replied.

"We all want to help. We take care of our own. We are family. No one is going to stay quiet on this. If anyone had info, they would tell you," Lady said.

"We're just so sorry we didn't see who she was talking to and that we couldn't get to her ourselves," Sheleeta added.

"We were just going into the Whip for a drink. Want to join us?" Laura asked.

"No, but thanks. We're on the clock," Lady said. "We'll keep our ears open."

"Among other things," Lady and Sheleeta said in unison, laughing.

"Let's get to work, little sister," Lady said.

"Time to earn some money with my outback steak-house," Sheleeta said.

They waved good-bye and walked away.

"That was a little more information than I wanted," Laura said.

Slick just laughed.

They turned to go, but before entering the bar, Slick spotted a man in a tan overcoat across the street. He seemed to be looking at her very intently. When he saw Slick looking back at him, he quickly turned away and walked in the opposite direction.

"What is it?" Laura asked.

"I just saw someone. He was oddly familiar, and I had this sense of déjà vu."

# 22

Inside the Whip, the light was dim and the music wasn't throbbing yet. There were a few women at the bar and clusters of chatting women at several tables having lunch.

Slick and Laura found an empty table, and it wasn't long before a scantily clad waitress approached them to take their order.

"Two Absolut martinis, please, straight up," Slick said.

"Would you like them dirty?" the woman asked, winking.

"No, thanks," Laura said. "Just your basic classic martini, light on the vermouth and extra olives."

"You got it, babe." She smiled sweetly. She made a point to flirt with both of them, not knowing who was paying the check.

Slick looked around the bar. "I can't remember the last time we were here. Can you?

"No. They've made so many changes. I love how they've renovated," Laura said.

"Apparently they haven't made enough changes; they'll still let anybody in."

They turned toward the voice. It was Devlyn O'Hare.

She sat down with her drink, without waiting to be invited.

"Devlyn, what are you doing here?" Laura asked.

"Just doing a little foundation research. Newark is in the process of revitalizing, and I thought there may be some effort we could get involved with."

"Good idea. Find anything yet?" Laura asked.

"Not yet. Still canvassing. I just stopped in for a drink." Then she turned her attention to Slick. "Hello, Slick," Devlyn said. Her contempt was barely disguised behind a smile so sweet it could have been poured on pancakes. "How long has it been?"

"Not nearly long enough."

The waitress came with the martinis.

"Perfect timing; I really need this now," Slick said, looking at Devlyn.

"Laura, are you coming to the fund-raiser for Hyacinth House?" Devlyn asked.

Laura started to say no, but the look on Slick's face was urging her to go. "Yes, I guess so. I'll be there," she said.

"Wonderful, Laura. It will be like old times. You and me hosting a fund-raiser together like we used to. Working the room, shaming people into donating their money for those worthy causes."

"I never shamed anyone, Devlyn. Everyone has a better nature. I just tapped into that."

"Did I say shame?" Devlyn laughed. "What I meant to say is that I remind these rich people that their friends and family are not immune from horrible diseases, and freak accidents can happen to anyone."

"That's wrong and cruel."

Devlyn knew she should feel something, but she didn't. *Wrong* and *Cruel* were her two favorite words. "Oh, what the hell," she said. "We'll raise oodles of money. There's a lot of zeros in oodles. You'll be happy to know that contributions in general have been on the rise."

"There are more important things than money, Devlyn."

"Yes, there's power, but enough money can buy you power."

"I'm talking about integrity," Laura said, shaking her head. "I'll definitely be at the fund-raiser now to see that you're not coercing people for money."

"I'll be there, too, Devlyn," Slick said.

"You will? What a joy. I'm thrilled to my core. In fact, I'm going to make that my happy thought for the day," she said, giving a false smile that conveyed to Slick that she'd rather be at Omaha Beach on D-day.

Devlyn finished the last of her drink. "Well, I'll be going now. I should get back to work."

"Limo, or will the Flying Monkeys bring the broom around?" Slick asked.

Devlyn smiled ever so sweetly. "Have a wonderful day fighting crime, or whatever it is that you do. Oh, and just a reminder, Slick—the fund-raiser is a formal affair. Try to look only mildly horrifying."

A laugh bubbled up inside her, but Slick caught it before it blew past her lips. Devlyn was right. If Slick had her way, she'd spend her life in sweats and sneakers. But Slick wasn't going to give her the satisfaction.

"Good-bye, Laura."

After Devlyn had gone, Laura said, "I know my reasons for going to the fund-raiser, but what are yours?"

"We're not having a lot of success out here on the street

finding information on Gloria. Her clientele were rich. Maybe we'll get some leads there."

As they were leaving the Whip, the man Slick had seen before was back. She tried to get a better look at him.

"What is it?" Laura asked.

"We're being followed."

# 23

Slick and Laura entered the private party room of the Owen Charles Foundation building. It was the height of elegance, with multileveled seating and an outdoor patio. The hand-carved cherrywood bar and antique mirrors all conveyed the elegance of a bygone era.

Champagne was flowing, and black tuxedos and shimmering gowns were everywhere. There was lots of party chatter, and the harpist playing Mozart provided the perfect sound-track.

Servers wearing white gloves moved through the crowds with trays of canapés, jumbo shrimp, and assorted finger foods. Ice sculptures graced tables covered with fine imported linens.

"Nice crowd," Slick said.

"I'm guessing about two hundred people," Laura observed.

"Including Secret Service men and bodyguards," Slick added. She turned to Laura. "May I buy the head of the foundation a drink?"

"Why, of course."

They walked over to the bar, stopping along the way to

chat with a few local politicians, NBA players, and television personalities.

When they got to the bar, Slick asked for two glasses of champagne.

They clinked glasses and turned toward the crowd.

"You have to admit, Devlyn knows how to throw a party," Laura said, looking around.

"I'll give the devil her due," Slick agreed.

As if on cue, Devlyn made her entrance, spotted Laura, and started toward her like a heat-seeking missile.

"Laura, darling, you look wonderful." She gave Laura the perfunctory air-kiss.

"Slick," Devlyn said, unsmiling.

"Devlyn. So you really do wear Prada."

"Why, Slick, I'm surprised you know anything about designers," Devlyn said, looking her up and down.

"I know women with designs when I see them."

Devlyn quickly turned away. "Laura, you must make the rounds with me. We have to say hello and mingle. You don't mind, do you, Slick?"

"Not at all."

"Come with us, Slick," Laura said.

"No, I'll stay here. You go. You have to. It's your family's foundation."

"I'm sure Slick will be fine." Devlyn was beaming at the idea of having Laura to herself.

Slick finished her champagne and watched as Devlyn guided Laura through the crowd and directly toward the star of the evening, senatorial candidate Clinton Kendall.

Slick watched from across the room and did a quick appraisal of Kendall.

He was the perfect candidate. Six feet tall. Good-looking.

In great shape. About one hundred and seventy pounds, probably not much more than his college weight.

Kendall was old money. He wore his family pedigree comfortably. Right schools, right marriage to the former Elizabeth Kenilworth. A self-assured smile that attracted people. Even though the fund-raiser was for Hyacinth House, Kendall was clearly the center of attention.

Slick watched as Devlyn introduced Laura to Kendall, his wife, and his son. Then Devlyn and Laura moved on to chat with others. Slick thought she recognized some newscasters from the New Jersey News Channel.

"Are you Cassandra Slick?"

Slick looked around and saw a man standing next to her. He was medium height with glasses and was wearing a tuxedo that he looked terribly uncomfortable in.

"Yes, I am. And you are Howard Whitley, Kendall's campaign manager."

He seemed flattered. "I didn't think anyone paid much attention to me."

"I follow politics," Slick said. "I've seen you on some of the Sunday morning talk shows promoting Kendall. You took time off from your law practice to work for him."

"Yes, I did. He's the real deal." Whitley looked across the room at Kendall. "He's going to be the next senator from New Jersey."

"How do you know me?" Slick asked.

"When I was a lawyer, you arrested some of my former clients."

Slick laughed.

"Seriously, I keep up with what's going on. For example, I know you're looking into the murder of a prostitute and that one of your suspects is a police officer named Tom Brandeal." Slick must have looked a little startled, because he said, "Look, I was a defense attorney. We kept up with which cops were good and which were not. I know about the Sean MacGuire case. I know you worked that case with Brandeal."

Slick squirmed at the mention of the case but listened intently as Whitley continued. "Many of us felt the evidence against him was planted. Kendall wants to get rid of cops like Brandeal. He is the poster boy for cops gone bad. I hope you are pursuing him vigorously. Kendall wants to look into police corruption. I know he would want to meet you. Let me introduce you."

Whitley wouldn't take no for an answer and practically pushed Slick through the crowd to Kendall.

When they reached Kendall, Whitley whispered something in his ear; then Kendall flashed his best politician's smile at Slick. "Nice to meet you. I have heard of you. You have a great reputation at all levels of law enforcement," he said.

"Thank you," Slick said. "I've been following your campaign. Good luck."

"I hope I can count on your vote," Kendall said charmingly.

Whitley's cell phone rang, saving Slick from responding to Kendall.

"Excuse me, I have to take this," he said. "Hello. Yes, we'll take ten of the twenty-second spots. Those will go to which channels? Great."

Whitley clicked off, ending the conversation, and glanced around at the crowd. "I'm getting looks. I got to keep Kendall circulating. Good luck on your investigation."

"Thank you," Slick said. She watched as Whitley maneuvered Kendall and his family around the room. She was trying to see where Laura was when she spotted Devlyn heading to the podium.

"Thank you all for joining us tonight. Because of your contributions, we have been able to help a wide variety of charities, as well as social and artistic endeavors. This year we look forward to even greater success. We here at the Owen Charles Foundation appreciate your time and generosity. May I introduce the founder of the Owen Charles Foundation, Miss Laura Charles."

There was an outburst of applause as Laura walked to the microphone.

"Thank you," she said. "As you know, New Jersey's Hyacinth House provides a broad range of services for people affected by HIV. And since the impact of HIV extends beyond the people with the virus, Hyacinth House provides training services to community-based and professional organizations. Last year they provided direct services to over twenty thousand people. I am honored to host this evening for such a worthy cause."

From across the room, Clinton Kendall shouted, "Let me start off the evening with a check for five thousand dollars."

"Let me match that with a check for five thousand dollars."

Every head turned in the direction of the second voice.

It was Pete Moreno. Slick hadn't seen him earlier, so she assumed he must have come in while everyone's attention was on Laura.

The room erupted in applause for the two political rivals coming together for such a worthy cause.

Smiling, the two politicians met and shook hands in the center of the room. Flash bulbs went off, and Slick was sure the picture would be on the front page of tomorrow's *Star Ledger*.

*Well done by both politicians,* she thought. Slick saw Laura making her way through the crowd toward her and smiled at her proudly. "I'd say tonight will be a big success. Congratulations."

"Thank you. I hope so. Hyacinth does so much good work," Laura said.

Before they could continue, a woman took hold of Laura's arm.

"Laura, my name is Susan Harris. I'm from the Children's Wish Foundation. I'd like to set up something for us in May, as soon as possible. After this evening, I'm sure you're going to get requests from a lot of charities. Is it possible to book it tonight?"

Normally Laura would have had Devlyn book this, but Devlyn was busy talking with the governor.

"Certainly. Please come with me." Laura squeezed Slick's hand and said, "I'll be right back."

Laura and Susan left the party room and took an elevator to the foundation's offices.

Laura entered the code for Devlyn's office, went to her desk, and took out the master schedule for events.

"What day did you have in mind?" Laura asked.

"May tenth," Susan said.

"Yes, that day is available. We'll be in touch to work out the specifics."

"Oh, thank you, Laura! Thank you for booking tonight. I think we'll raise lots of money. I know you want to get back to the fund-raiser. I'll see myself out." Susan left in a hurry.

Laura was touched by her enthusiasm.

She was replacing the schedule when she saw something

else that caught her attention. Thinking it may have been some supplemental information, Laura opened it and started paging through it.

She was shocked.

Inside were names of some very prominent people with very graphic descriptions of their sexual penchants. A few of the doctors, politicians, and local television news celebrities were downstairs now, with their wives, drinking champagne in their tuxedos, eating shrimp and listening to Mozart, pledging money for Hyacinth House.

Most notably, there was Clinton Kendall's name.

Laura wondered how she was going to reenter the party room maintaining her composure. How could she talk with any of them? It was as if she had just seen these people naked.

Earlier, Devlyn had been bragging that the contributions would be going up. Is this how she was getting the money?

Laura was horrified; she felt faint and dropped into Devlyn's chair.

What would be the future of her foundation?

"Oh, my God," Laura said out loud. "What have you done now, Devlyn?"

# 24

It was the doorman's first day on the job. The others before him had been fired because they were not quick enough. Yes, he had to let people in and out, be polite, help with packages, but his first priority was to be on the lookout for her.

He gazed up at the twenty-story Owen Charles Foundation and wondered what scared them. It was a beautiful foundation that raised and gave money to needy, sick, or artistic people.

Jose looked up the street and saw a long stretch limo approaching. It stopped directly in front of the building. The sight of it held him momentarily still.

The driver got out and, standing at attention, opened the door for the passenger. Jose watched as a fabulously shaped leg set in a Jimmy Choo emerged from the open door. The door closed, and he heard the crunch of footsteps. The woman approached, looking only straight ahead.

Jose started to say good morning and tip his hat, but she stopped, dropped her sunglasses, and gave him a look that almost seared the flesh from his face.

"You're new," she said.

"Yes, Miss . . . um . . . Thank you for this opportu—"

"You're short," she said.

"Yes, I am a little person in a big world, but I can still—"

"Shouldn't you be announcing the plane, Tattoo?" She turned away and headed into the building.

"*Ay, Dios mio,*" Jose exclaimed as he frantically made the sign of the cross.

He tried to compose himself, and his eyes drifted to the limo driver, who was trying to signal him, arms and legs flapping and flailing.

"Hurry! Call them! Call them!"

"Santa Maria!" Jose exclaimed.

He pressed the little red button.

Jose couldn't see what was going on behind him inside the building, but as soon as he pressed the little red button, people fled for cover behind cabinets, into supply closets, and under desks.


When she entered the lobby, the elevator was there for her, but the people who had been standing there waiting for it had all fled, scrambling in every direction, some opting to take the stairs, others to escape through windows.

She stepped in all alone, the doors slid closed, and the elevator started to rise. When it was certain she was gone, people slowly came from out of their hiding places, not unlike the Munchkins timidly investigating their surroundings after Dorothy landed on the Wicked Witch.

When the elevator doors opened on her floor, she stepped out into the carpeted hall. People heading toward the elevator quickly turned around and ran away. As she walked past, everyone working nearby noticed her. Phone conversations stopped, heads turned, and eyes popped. Fingers on keyboards that had been clacking along rapidly froze in midstroke. Staff members were alerted that Miss O'Hare was present.

"Good morning, Miss O'Hare."

She was greeted by a woman standing at attention, shaking and terror-stricken.

"Shall I have some coffee sent in for you?"

"I have nonstop meetings throughout the day, important conferences with important people. Of course I want coffee."

Devlyn keyed in her office code number, opened the door, and stepped inside.

"Tell me about the diary, Devlyn."

# 25

Laura's voice startled Devlyn, but before she turned around, Devlyn recovered quickly and put on her best smile.

"Laura, always good to see you. And Slick. What are you doing in my chair?"

"I wanted a front-row seat for what's about to happen," Slick said, smiling slyly.

Devlyn looked at her curiously.

Laura crossed to her quickly and got in her face. She was furious and was holding the diary in front of Devlyn's nose. "Is this your diary?" Laura demanded.

"No."

"Then explain why I found it in your desk."

"I can explain—"

"Have you been cataloging our contributors' sexual behavior, then blackmailing them for money, for donations?"

Devlyn appeared shocked. "Of course not!"

"Devlyn, if you're lying . . ." Laura took a menacing step forward.

It always amazed Devlyn how fast Laura's soft features grew steely when she was angry. Devlyn knew to take her seriously. "I'm not lying, I swear. In fact, the diary came in the mail."

Laura looked skeptical.

Behind Laura, Devlyn could see that Slick was smirking, looking not even vaguely convinced she was telling the truth.

"Come on, Devlyn, you can do better than that," Laura said coldly.

"It did come in the mail—addressed to you, Laura."

"Me?"

"Yes. The outside envelope was addressed to you here." Devlyn's voice trailed off a bit. "The inside envelope had Slick's name on it."

"What?" Slick shot up from the chair.

"Yes, there was a note inside. It was signed Gloria something."

Slick and Laura exchanged a brief look.

"Do you still have the note?" Laura asked.

"No, I threw it out."

"Why didn't you say something?" Slick asked.

Devlyn ignored Slick's question. "Laura, you know you're rarely here. We agreed that I would open all mail addressed to you here at the foundation. I didn't know if this diary was real or who sent it. I didn't know what to think. The day I ran into you at the Whip, I was checking it out for damage control, just in case it was real. I was only trying to protect the good name of your foundation and our contributors. I was not blackmailing anyone."

"Not yet," Slick muttered.

"Why, it never entered my mind," Devlyn protested.

"I'd ask you to swear to that on a bible, but I have this image of your flesh starting to sizzle and smoke if it ever came in touch with something holy," Laura said.

"It hurts me that you don't believe me. I am so misunderstood." Devlyn's eyes welled and she squeezed out a single tear.

Slick was incredulous. She rolled her eyes so far back she could see her own hair growing.

"So, then, what did you do?" Laura pressed.

"Well, I called Pete Moreno and asked if he wanted the info on Kendall."

"Did you ask Moreno for money?"

"No."

"Then what was in it for you?"

"Any little consideration he might have after he won the election to the Senate. But he turned me down."

"Damn it, Devlyn!"

"Oh, now, Laura, you know it can't hurt to have some friends in high places. Nothing wrong with that. I was only thinking that people love politicians and celebrities. They like having their pictures taken with them. If we could get whoever won—Moreno or Kendall—to come to two or three fund-raisers a year, it would be good for us, good for our causes. Big names attract people."

"And what about Kendall? What did he do when you called him?"

"I made the same offer to him, but he turned me down, too. The only person interested in it was Howard Whitley. He didn't want it to harm Kendall's campaign. But he wasn't interested in it anymore."

"Still, I don't like the idea of you using these politicians."

"I wasn't using them. They would agree to lend their names to a worthy cause, show up here and get some good press. It was a win-win situation for us and for them."

"But you were brokering information."

"I let both parties know that there was damaging information. I didn't release it to the press. Whatever they did with the information was up to them."

Laura studied her face, trying to sort through her story. She had no proof that Devlyn was lying. And a representative from Hyacinth House had called Laura directly at her home to thank her for their most successful fund-raiser to date.

Devlyn knew Laura was deep in thought and knew it was wise to take the focus off her. "So, Slick, who is this Gloria, anyway, an old girlfriend?"

Slick's expression clouded.

Devlyn knew she had hit her mark and gave a satisfied smile. "My, my, my. I'm right, aren't I? You were in love with her. There were a lot of men in that diary, Slick. I mean, a whole lot of men."

"Enough, Devlyn," Laura said.

But Devlyn didn't stop. "Was she your first? Apparently your masterly lesbian touch ushered Gloria into heterosexual happiness. Oh, the pride you must feel."

"I said that's enough, Devlyn."

"In fact, I'd say she was a blissfully happy hetero. Not much of a dream date, were you? Watch out, Laura, you may suddenly become straight."

"You watch out, Devlyn," Laura warned. "If I find out you did do something wrong . . ."

"I understand," Devlyn said contritely, "but I didn't do anything more than I told you."

Laura turned to go.

Now it was Devlyn smirking over Laura's shoulder at Slick.

"Okay, Laura, let's go," Slick said.

They left and closed the door to the office behind them, Devlyn's laughter audible from inside.

"She could be telling the truth," Laura said.

"Or she could have gotten Gloria's name on Halsey Street and written up some dirt on people."

"There are a lot of entries in that diary."

"So?"

"Devlyn isn't the type to spend that much time inventing things."

Slick had to agree. "We have to validate the authenticity of the diary. That it really came from Gloria," she said.

"Are we going to see Moreno or Kendall to check out Devlyn's story?"

"Neither," Slick answered. "Not yet. There was one name in the diary that interests me more right now."

# 26

"I need a word with you."

Captain DeStasio looked up from his desk, surprised at her entry. Slick had never come into his office without knocking and in such obvious agitation.

"Of course," he said. "Come in," he added unnecessarily. Slick was not about to be kept from entering. Once in, she closed the door behind her more firmly than was necessary.

She planted herself firmly in front of DeStasio's desk. "Anything you want to tell me?"

"Detective?"

"Do you want to explain why your name appears on Paradise's clientele list as a regular customer?"

For a moment, he didn't have the foggiest idea what she was talking about and could only sit there gaping at her, feeling exquisitely stupid.

Slick slammed the diary onto DeStasio's desk. "I learned way more than I ever wanted to know about you. Plus you're a lousy tipper."

Then he understood entirely. The captain just looked at the journal for several moments without speaking. "So. She really did keep a diary," he said finally. "She never told me. Some said she did, some said she didn't. I always wondered. It makes sense. A good call girl sees six hundred to seven hundred clients a year. Faces get blurred."

Slick was silent, waiting for him to continue.

DeStasio saw her questioning expression. "It's a long story," he said.

"Okay, I'm listening."

"No. You're not."

He was right. Slick paced back and forth in front of his desk, remembering all the assignments she had gotten, all the times she had asked for advice, all the little bits of wisdom and insight DeStasio had shared with her. She had trusted him, looked up to him, loved his tolerance and patience, and most of all she loved his dogged belief in what was right and what was wrong.

Even now, while she was dangerously close to saying something disrespectful that she'd probably regret later, his eyes looked patiently at her.

"I see you're upset."

"You think? What gave me away?"

DeStasio ignored the eruption and remained patient. "Can I get you something? Coffee or soda?"

"No."

"You need to calm down, Slick. Collect your thoughts."

"Trust me, my thoughts are pretty focused."

"Then have a seat, Detective."

"No."

The captain managed to control his rush of anger, but just barely.

"I said have a seat, goddammit, so put your ass in the chair."

This time Slick did as she was told and settled herself in the chair in front of DeStasio's desk, staring him in the eye.

DeStasio was silent.

"Well?"

He didn't know where to begin. Struggling to find the right words, he picked up the picture of his wife and looked at it tenderly. "She was beautiful when we got married. I wouldn't change a thing about that day. We were twenty-nine years old, and we had the rest of our lives ahead of us." His voice was soft, almost caressing. "Over the years, she got a little gray, got a few lines around the eyes. I liked it. She was still beautiful when she died and it nearly finished me. I don't remember the days leading up to the funeral, who organized the arrangements, found the funeral director. It all seemed so unreal until I went to get something out of a closet, where I found her favorite purse. I opened it and emptied it onto the floor and burst into tears. I sat there touching the litter from her purse. The Kleenex, the Lifesavers, the little bottle of Purell, her keys.

"I miss having her to talk to. For the longest time, the simplest things of everyday life seemed impossible. When I'd come home from work, I'd miss the smell of her preparing dinner as I walked in the door. Sitting on the couch to watch TV wasn't the same. I even missed stupid little things like her constantly reminding me to pay the paperboy.

"I can still remember our honeymoon. It was moonlight and roses and all the stuff you hear about. I can still remember how she smelled and how her body felt so soft in my arms."

Slick squirmed uncomfortably in her chair. She knew her hard-boiled captain had a soft heart, but she hadn't realized how powerfully his wife's death had affected him. She wondered if this was the first time he had spoken of his grief to someone. Men like him rarely did. Slick's face relaxed a little from its hard position. She kept her eyes from his and let them drift over the familiar things in his office.

"We were young. Nothing in this world could separate us. Then she was gone, and everything that we had seemed like a dream. I realized then that what we had was like a piece of fine glass that you protect. When it got smashed . . ." He put down the picture. "Memories hurt," he said, "especially the good ones. Think about them too much and you'll go nuts."

Slick held up the diary. "How long have you been doing this?"

"I stopped seeing Paradise over three years ago. I wasn't looking for it. My wife had been dead for five years. A part of me died with her. I belong to an exclusive gentlemen's club." DeStasio paused. "Gentlemen's club. Saying it out loud now makes it sound absurd. They all were involved with her."

"I guess membership really does have its privileges," Slick said.

"I know I had other options, other ways to go besides finding a pros, but this was so personal. Gloria understood that."

"Make me understand that."

An angry look flashed momentarily in DeStasio's eyes. "I don't have to justify myself to you. I don't need you to absolve me of my sins. Everybody's life has twists. Don't assume you have all the answers. You don't."

"Why didn't you tell me before?"

"It's a little hard to tell the people you command that you're involved with a prostitute." DeStasio got up from his chair and sat on the edge of his desk in front of Slick. "Look, you've got me admitting to being with a prostitute. You can walk away now and give whatever information you have on me to IAB. I've been telling myself that I didn't go to IAB because I still think Brandeal didn't kill her, and why put us both in jeopardy if he's innocent. But I broke the law and I broke protocol. I won't deny it, and I will understand if you give me up."

"I don't mean any disrespect, Captain. You know I don't."

"I know that, Detective."

"I apologize for my bad behavior."

"Is there anything else?"

"Did you kill her?" Her eyes locked on his.

Something like a smile skimmed across his lips. The pointedness of the question shouldn't have surprised him. Of course she was going to ask.

"If I did, do you think I'd get you involved?"

"That's not an answer, sir."

DeStasio made his shoulders very square and correct.

"No, Detective, I did not kill her. I would never do anything to hurt her. The last thing I said to the senator at the club who was leading the effort to kill her is that I would bring him to justice if he harmed her. I meant to keep that promise. I can't be any clearer than that. When I found out that Brandeal was using her for a snitch, I was relieved. I thought he could protect her. I still think he's innocent, but maybe someone got to Brandeal and turned him against her. I want to know for certain if Brandeal killed her or not."

"Do you have anyone else you suspect?"

"No."

Slick rose from her chair and began to pace, her head bowed in thought.

"What's the name of the senator who was going to have her killed?"

"That would be Senator Wilson Lovett."

She stopped in her tracks. "Senator Lovett? He died two years ago."

"That's right. You see, Gloria changed her mind again. She did that several times before she actually quit."

"Would there be anyone at this gentlemen's club who would step up and act on Senator Lovett's threat?"

DeStasio laughed quietly. "No. Most of the men there are so old now, they would welcome a little sex scandal."

"Is Clinton Kendall a member of your club?"

"Kendall? No. Not that I know of. I've never seen him there. We've never met."

"Did Brandeal know about your involvement with Gloria?"

"It's possible, but I don't think so. I can't swear that he doesn't know, but it's not Gloria's style to talk about her clients. The only reason I know some of the men she was involved with is because they talked about it at the club."

"Okay, then," Slick said. "I've asked and you've answered."

"Do you believe me?"

"I want to believe, sir."

"Fair enough. I'll take that for now, Detective."

"Any more surprises?" Slick asked.

"Not from me." DeStasio looked at her closely. "Now it's my turn to ask some questions. What's going on? This is about more than you finding my name in a book."

Slick looked suddenly sad. DeStasio waited quietly. "Paradise . . . Gloria was a friend of mine. Years ago in school."

"I'm sorry."

"I had lost touch with her, and now she's dead. I guess I took some of my anger out on you. I apologize."

"I'm sorry you had to find out about my involvement with her this way."

"I guess there are different levels of wrong. You're not the same as the men who were just using her. You're better than them, Captain. I believe you really cared for her."

Slick put her hand on his shoulder. She had never done that before, but neither of them noticed.

# 27

Bernice Roxley opened the door of her little home and almost fainted. She looked at the face of the one little girl who had always been a friend to her daughter. In those fleeting seconds, time reversed itself.

"Cassandra Slick. Cassandra Slick." So much affection in those words.

"Hi, Mrs. Roxley," Slick said.

"I'm glad you've come," she said. "It's been a long time." She hugged Slick tightly, and Slick felt immediately guilty for not visiting sooner. "Look at you, all grown up, Cassie. And a police officer, too. I've read about you in the papers."

"I'm here about Gloria."

"She's gone, Cassie," Mrs. Roxley said softly.

"I'm so sorry this happened."

The old woman's eyes were puffy and red rimmed. When she inhaled, there was a distinct slushy and moist sound from inside her.

Slick stepped inside and felt like she was stepping back in time. So little had changed since she'd last been inside these walls. She could almost hear echoes of herself and Gloria laughing as they ran playing inside, could almost smell bacon, eggs, and grits on the stove, her favorite breakfast that Mrs. Roxley would make when she slept over. She could almost smell Gloria.

On the walls were pictures and mementoes, dusty and tattered. The house looked the same, but it felt emptier. A feeling of aching loss was heavy in the air. Bernice sat in her rocker and stared dully at the wall. Her voice broke into Slick's thoughts.

"I knew you'd come, Cassie. Introduce me to your friend, then sit down."

Mrs. Roxley shushed her cat off the couch. It jumped to the windowsill, then sat motionless, except for its twitching tail. Slick obediently did as she was told.

Mrs. Roxley still spoke to her the way someone speaks to a lovable but inexperienced child. Apparently, Mrs. Roxley still felt that Slick hadn't yet reached the turning point of their adult–child relationship.

Bernice Roxley had always been a strong woman of good health and faith. Outliving her husband and now her daughter, she looked frail and strained, yet somehow she pushed on with the dignity of her age.

"I feel you looking at me, Cassie. I got the cancer. I've been given about six months. Death is near me now. It whispers in my ear in the dark. But I decided no chemo, no surgery. I'm so old, the treatment would probably kill me, so why bother? I'm ready to go whenever the Good Lord calls me."

"Are you in any pain?"

"No, I got my pills."

"Are you all alone here? Is someone looking after you?"

"Don't you worry about me, Cassandra. I got plenty of people looking in after me." Then she stirred and pulled herself up out of her rocker. "And I ain't so old as to forget my manners. Let me fix you two some tea."

Slick and Laura started to protest but soon realized they weren't going to talk her out of it.

"There will be no feeling sorry for me allowed in this house."

"Well, can I at least help you?" Slick asked.

"I'd never refuse a little help," she said, then added, "but you just sit still, Laura. This is your first time in my home, and you're my guest."

"Yes, ma'am," Laura said. As Slick and Mrs. Roxley disappeared into the kitchen, she looked around the house with its photos of Gloria as a child, when the house was filled with happier times.

After a while, they returned from the kitchen with Slick carrying a tray with cups, saucers, sugar, cream, and lemon slices.

"Let's have our tea here," Mrs. Roxley said, pointing to the couch table. Laura moved the pillows and Slick put the tray down. Mrs. Roxley went back to the kitchen and returned with the teapot and a plate of cookies.

"Sorry, these are store bought. I don't bake like I used to."

She set the pot and cookies down, then sat in her rocker. The cat jumped off the window and curled up at her feet. "I have lots of time now to think back on things. Gloria was my heart. I kept asking God to put her back right, to get her out of that life. It never happened. It took me a long time to find my way back to him."

A deep sadness invaded her face.

"And now she's dead. When I went to identify her, I had to walk down a long corridor with green tiles on the wall. I was thinking it was the ugliest shade of green I had ever seen.

How could my little girl be in such an ugly place? Then they rolled her out. It was impossible to look at her, but it was impossible to look away. So I looked at her there on that table, seeing her but not believing. I could not connect my baby to that dead body. I kept trying to touch her through the glass. I try not to think of her that way, but I know I'll go on seeing her there, whether I'm awake or asleep, for a long time to come."

Slick knew that would be the case. She had seen enough lifeless bodies to know that the dead never look like they're only sleeping. That story was probably invented to comfort little children. Without life inside, the human body looked like the flat compilation of parts it was.

Seeing Gloria dead would eclipse a thousand memory pictures that Mrs. Roxley had of Gloria when she was alive. Whatever words of sympathy or comfort Slick wanted to say, no matter how deeply felt, would only sound hollow. So she said nothing.

Slick was very grateful now to have the tea in front of her. She couldn't look in Mrs. Roxley's eyes just then; the transfer of pain would have been brutal. So Slick feigned an urgent need for more tea and refilled her cup as she began to ask the old woman questions.

Maybe Mrs. Roxley understood, because she averted her gaze, not wishing to draw anyone into the misery her eyes revealed.

"When did you last see her . . . before . . ."

"Oh, she was so happy, looking forward to her life with Tommy. That's all she talked about."

"Tommy? Who's Tommy?" Slick asked.

"I don't know his last name. Someone she knew."

"You mind if we look around?"

"Go ahead, but the house was searched yesterday."

"Yesterday? By who?"

"Detective Brandeal."

Slick and Laura did a cursory search of the house and found nothing. Gloria had not lived there in a while.

Before they left, Mrs. Roxley hugged them both tightly and made Slick and Laura promise they would visit her again.

As they walked toward their car, the man who had been following them lit a cigarette. When they drove away, he started his car and took off after them.

# 28

Tom Brandeal unlocked the door to his home. He put his keys, gun, and badge on the dining room table, then walked directly to the cabinet where he kept his scotch. He took the bottle to the kitchen, threw some ice in a glass, and poured himself a drink. It wasn't his first one for the day, and he knew it wouldn't be his last.

He removed the package from his jacket pocket. It was a security tape. He walked over to his television and slipped the tape into the VCR. For the longest time, there was nothing of interest to him, just people and animals coming and going through Echo Lake Park.

With one hand, he picked up the remote and fast-forwarded the tape; with the other hand, he tossed back some scotch.

When he finally got to the section he wanted, he sat up straight and watched attentively. There he was, caught on tape in Echo Lake Park. The quality wasn't the greatest, and he wasn't certain that the tape could be used to positively identify him, especially since the cowboy hat concealed most of his face.

The tape continued to play, and then Tom Brandeal saw

the bastard with the cell phone and his dog who had chased him in the park. He wondered why the guy hadn't come forward yet and talked to police. Brandeal drank some more scotch. It was possible that he hadn't seen Brandeal dump the car and didn't make the connection to the murder. If the guy ever did come forward, this could be used as evidence.

Brandeal's glass was nearly empty. He got up and poured himself more scotch and decided there was only one thing he could do.

He picked up the remote and erased that portion of the tape. He rewound it to make sure that section had been wiped clean. When he replayed it, there was nothing there but static.

Brandeal finished his drink, and it was starting to get to him. He did not turn off the VCR, and through his drunken fog, he saw something that could finally get him out of his private hell.

# 29

Slick and Laura walked down the path to Echo Lake. It was a beautiful fall night in Mountainside, with autumn leaves kicking along the ground propelled by a soft feathery wind. A woman on a bicycle with a flickering headlamp, a dog running alongside, passed them and smiled. The park had a sense of quiet. It may as well have been early spring. People were out dressed in T-shirts and shorts. Winter seemed distant.

Deer crept to the edge of the park and nibbled on leaves. They stopped, looked up, then, not feeling threatened, went back to their nibbling.

It seemed unthinkable that only days before this, a dead body was found in this setting.

They walked to the north edge of the lake where the car containing Gloria's remains had been found. In the distance, some swimmers who had been cavorting in the water splashed their way to shore, dried themselves off, walked to the bikes they had left leaning against the trees nearby, and pedaled away, the sounds of their laughter disappearing with them. The lake was still again.

Slick walked back and forth, studying the area. She checked

the area thoroughly to make sure they were in the exact spot. "This doesn't make sense," she said.

"What doesn't?"

"This is the shallow end of the lake. You can't submerge a car here. So why did the killer drive the car here?"

"Maybe he didn't know that," Laura said. "Maybe he just panicked."

"Maybe, but if I wanted to dispose of a body in water, I'd make sure the water was deep enough. Otherwise, what's the point?"

They continued to check the scene for other evidence.

There was a full moon out, but it was hidden now behind a rolling bank of clouds.

In the distance, barely audible at first but growing louder was the sound of car tires rolling over stones. They both heard it. In the dark, it was vague and directionless.

Then Slick got her bearings and pointed. It was coming from the upper end of the private road opposite the way Slick and Laura had entered the park off Route 22.

The sound of the car engine grew even closer. There was no other noise. Not even crickets. No headlights or even a hint of them could be seen. Abruptly the sound ceased and the night was noiseless again.

Then they could hear the car door open.

Slick and Laura moved slowly in the copse of trees, using the darkness for cover, trying to see who was driving. When they could see the car, they stood perfectly still, watching and listening, no sound but their own breathing.

At that moment, the moon came out from behind the cloud bank. It was a solo beacon, making them visible in the white lunar light.

The driver must have spotted them, because the car door

opened and closed, then came the sound of rapidly acceler-
ated tires bearing down, wildly spraying rocks and gravel as it
sped away, careening into the night.

"Did you see who it was?" Laura asked.

"No, but I have a new respect for Homeland Security,"
Slick said, pointing up into the trees.

# 30

Slick and Laura walked up to the visitors' center in Echo Park. It was a log building nearly obscured by pines and evergreens. The interior was paneled in a coffee-colored wood and contained a one-room bookstore to the left, bathrooms to the right, and a breezeway in between.

There was a long polished pine counter with a gleaming railing set with a gate separating the public from the park staff.

Slick and Laura went to the counter, and they were met by a darkly tanned woman. Her brown hair was cut short and gelled back. Her manner was very no-nonsense.

"I'm here to see Ranger Cleavon," Slick said.

"That would be me. How can I help you?"

Slick showed her detective badge. Ranger Cleavon inspected it closely and was impressed. Her smile was genuine. "Always glad to help out a fellow officer," she said.

"I understand you have surveillance cameras in the park?"

"Yes, we do," she said proudly.

"How does that work?"

"Come with me and I'll show you." Ranger Cleavon opened the little gate and let them in.

Slick and Laura followed her into the inner office. It was a typical little government office that made do with whatever was left over from funding other agencies. It was small, equipped with an old metal desk and filing cabinets. The scuffed wooden floor was covered with a Navajo rug. Smoky Bear posters were on the wall. As they entered, she offered them coffee. They looked at the pot. It brewed four cups at a time. Both Slick and Laura declined the offer.

Then there was the console, which looked shiny, new, and expensive, and totally out of place.

Ranger Cleavon went to the console and touched it like a proud parent. "We have CCTV, closed-circuit television cameras, throughout the park, making it one of the safest places in the state. We get a lot of traffic in here, so the program started focusing on the parking lots. We have really cut down on the number of cars stolen here. So we did a little expansion to other areas of the park."

"Expansion?" Slick asked.

"Yes. We get arrests in the park from time to time," she explained. "You know, for lewd behavior, indecent exposure, some drug stuff."

"How many cameras do you have?" Laura asked.

"About sixteen. We're hoping to increase that number as we validate the usage of them."

"What about privacy? Can these tapes be used in court?" Slick asked.

Ranger Cleavon smiled broadly. "That's the beauty of our system. They don't have sound."

Laura didn't understand. "No sound? So what?"

"It's not eavesdropping," Ranger Cleavon explained. "There's no capturing of substantive oral communication."

"I get it," Slick said. "It's an open park, and there's no reasonable expectation of privacy, so anything that happens in the park is in full public view."

"That's right. The cameras have become a vital partner in our crime-fighting arsenal. Indispensable."

Slick and Laura exchanged a brief look.

She sounded more like a soldier guarding a remote outpost than a park ranger in one of the nicest sections of New Jersey.

"So, then, how can I help you?" the ranger asked.

"I'm looking for a tape you may have on Echo Lake," Slick said.

"Well, we don't have cameras viewing every single area of the park, but I can get you tape from the closest area. When did you have in mind?"

"This would have been shot around ten P.M. to midnight on Friday."

"You're talking about the body found in the lake. That little incident will probably make it possible for us to get the funding we want. Sure, everyone wants to keep the park clear of illegal drug traffic and lewd behavior, but now we have a murder and a body."

"Yes, we're investigating this with the police," Slick said.

Ranger Cleavon looked confused. "I thought you were here to investigate some other goings-on in the park."

"No, we're here for the car with the body found in it."

"Oh, yes, we did have tape on that."

"Well, can we see it?" Slick asked.

"That was already handed over to the police."

"When?"

Ranger Cleavon checked the tape log. "Two days ago," she said.

"Do you have a name?"

"Yes. Detective Tom Brandeal."

Ranger Cleavon started to give them the ticket number, but Slick and Laura had already left.

# 31

Slick's cell phone chirped as she and Laura were on their way to see Captain DeStasio. Slick didn't recognize the number of the caller, but she answered, anyway.

"Hello." There was no response, and the connection was bad. "Hello," she said again. This time louder.

"Is this Slick . . . Cassandra Slick?"

"Yes. Who are you?"

"I'm a friend of Gloria's. I got your number from her mother. Gloria trusted you. She said I could trust you."

Slick listened intently. "Do you have a name?"

"Do you have the journal?"

"Maybe."

"I need to talk to you. I know what happened to her."

"You've got my attention. Talk to me."

"My name is Marchinko, TJ. I used to be in the life with Gloria."

That's why the man in the tan overcoat looked familiar to her. It was Tommy Marchinko who Slick had seen outside the bar—Gloria's friend Tommy whom Mrs. Roxley said she was going away with.

"Marchinko, eh? I thought you were still locked up?"

"No, I'm out."

"How long?"

"I been out for a while now. Nearly three months."

"You must have a good lawyer," Slick commented.

"The best." Marchinko laughed. He sounded a little nervous, though.

"You've been following me," she said.

"Yes," he admitted. "I got something for you, and I wanted to make sure it was you. Then when I saw you asking questions about her on Halsey Street, I was certain she sent you the journal. Gloria wanted to get out of the life. We were going away together. She was with a lot of influential people, people who would not like it to get out that she was involved with them. Gloria told me she sent it to someone she trusted. These people want the journal. They want to destroy it. They will do anything to get it. Now my life is in danger, too."

"Is someone threatening you?"

"You paying attention to the upcoming election? Let's just say Clinton Kendall has a lot of interest in that diary. Can you help me?"

"No promises."

"You need me, Slick. I can verify that the diary is authentic, that it was Gloria's. I know what it looks like, a lot of what it contained—names, dates, preferences."

The connection was breaking up. Slick yelled at him to speak louder.

"Just bring the diary with you," he said loudly.

"How do I know it's really you, Marchinko? You're just a voice on my cell phone. These are influential men who wanted Gloria dead. How do I know this isn't a setup?"

"You used to be a police detective. Now you're free-lance."

Slicked laughed. "Anybody could know that. What else you got?"

"When Gloria sent you the diary, there was something in there known only to the two of you . . . 'promise not to tell.'"

Slick was silent. "Okay, I'm a believer. Where are you?"

"Let me give you the address where I'm staying before you lose me. I'll be alone."

Slick wrote it down. She knew where it was. It was a lost neighborhood, dark, dreary, and lately dangerous, alive with crime and forgotten people. Kids in gangs stealing cars and shooting dope and sometimes each other. Homeless winos dead to the world on the pavement. Life didn't mean much there.

Then Marchinko started shouting over the interference. Slick strained to listen.

"I was there when she was killed . . . Brandeal . . . he wrapped her body in the blankets . . . put her in the trunk . . . I saw him."

Then the connection was lost.

Slick took a turn and Laura looked surprised.

"Aren't we going to see DeStasio?" she asked.

"We're going to make another stop first. Maybe now I can nail Brandeal."

# 32

TJ Marchinko answered the knock at the door only to find a gun being pointed squarely in his face. Marchinko went ashen, surprised by the visit. He gasped and staggered back far enough into the room so that the man with the gun could enter and close the door behind him. All the while, the man's eyes never left Marchinko's face, and the gun remained aimed at his head.

Marchinko's mind raced, trying to think, trying to find a way out. He felt a cold sweat breaking across his forehead.

"Do you have the journal?" the man asked.

"Not yet."

"That's too bad. I need results. What good are you to me?" He spat the words out angrily.

Marchinko backed up cautiously. "Calm down. I'm working on it," he said. "I'll get it, I swear. It should be very soon now."

The man was still agitated. "Why should I believe you? Maybe you've got it already and you're thinking about using it to your advantage."

He moved in closer to Marchinko, putting the gun between his eyes.

"Let's just take it easy," Marchinko said nervously, his hands up over his head to show he was not resisting. "Let's take it nice and slow."

"Let's not. We need to talk."

The man poked Marchinko's forehead with the gun two times.

"I find I'm a lot more talkative without a gun staring me in the face."

The man with the gun smiled, but it wasn't very pleasant-looking. It was more like his face had cracked and split.

The chuckle that followed the smile was even less appealing. It sounded like bones rattling. Suddenly Marchinko was reminded of the sound of Gloria Roxley's neck breaking. How he had stood there doing nothing to help her while this man murdered her. He remembered the fear in her eyes. He wondered if he looked the same.

"I really had you going there for a minute, didn't I?" the man asked, bringing Marchinko back from his thoughts.

He winked and lowered the gun. "I'm not going to shoot you in the face."

TJ Marchinko laughed nervously and felt a little more at ease. "Yeah, that was pretty good. I really thought you were going to blow my head off."

"No, of course I wouldn't shoot you in the head. First, I'm going to shoot you in the knee."

Marchinko heard a pop and then his knee exploded. He looked down in amazement. He started to scream, but before he could, the man with the gun stuffed something into TJ's mouth, then drove a knee into his stomach. Marchinko toppled to the floor, trying to clutch what was left of his shattered right knee, uselessly trying to stop the blood that was gushing through his fingers.

Once Marchinko was down, the man moved quickly to tape his mouth shut.

"I don't think we want you screaming, do we?" he asked. Then he stepped back, watching Marchinko writhing on the floor, gasping for breath.

"This is a twenty-two," the man said, circling Marchinko as he thrashed about in agony, looking admiringly at the small-caliber weapon. "Some say it's a woman's gun, but it's a personal favorite of mine. What I love about it is that I can shoot you several times without killing you."

The man took aim. "See."

There was another pop and Marchinko's elbow shattered. His arm flopped at his side. Marchinko fell flat on his back as pain and fear engulfed him.

"Are you working with anyone?" The man took aim at TJ's ankle.

Marchinko rapidly shook his head no and tried to say it through the small towel that was stuffed in his mouth. His eyes were wide, and his breathing was rapid and shallow.

"Why do I think you're lying?" the man asked tauntingly. Again Marchinko shook his head no.

"If there are others, you'd better tell me now."

NONONONONONO!

The man was convinced Marchinko was telling the truth. But he had one more question. "Have you told Slick about your connection to me?" He ground the gun into the flesh between Marchinko's ankle and heel.

"NO! NO! NO! NO! I SWEAR!" he tried to say, knowing the man couldn't understand him. All he could do was continue to shake his head frantically. Perspiration was running down his face.

Marchinko thought about his phone call to Slick. He was in brutal pain, but he was not yet despairing. *I am still alive,* he thought. He forced himself to focus on his meeting with Slick. She might get there in time to save him and stop this maniac.

Marchinko dug his fingers into the thinning carpet, clawing and tearing at it as if getting a firm hold on it might also give him the power to cling to his life and stop it from dwindling away, to keep his terror from slipping into madness. He still had hope that he'd survive. . . .

Until . . .

"What's that?" The man was cupping his ear. "What did you say? I'm sorry, I didn't quite catch that. I can't understand you when your mouth is full. *Have you told Slick about your connection to me?*"

Practically hysterical, Marchinko shook his head no.

The man with the gun seemed pleased at this news and smiled. He encouraged Marchinko to smile, too. Marchinko tried as best he could. For a heartbeat, he felt a twinge of hope that he'd survive.

"Well, maybe you haven't told her yet, but you will tell her eventually. I know you. You wouldn't be able to stand the pressure. I'm afraid I can't take that chance. So, you see, you've become a liability to me. If you're dead, you can't connect anyone to the journal."

The man shot out Marchinko's foot.

Marchinko knew it was over. His time had run out. He wasn't going to make it off the floor alive. Tears ran down his face, fast and unstoppable. The pain seared through him, closing in, crushing and suffocating him. If his mouth hadn't been taped, his screams would have shattered the windows. Now he begged for the mercy of being shot in the head.

The man with the gun understood his muffled pleas. He envisioned Marchinko's mouth moving like a dying fish behind the tape. He got close to Marchinko's face and whispered in his ear. "Kill you? Sure, if you insist." He chuckled. "This is where I came in, isn't it? We're right back where we started from, aren't we? Do you appreciate the irony of that? I'm going to miss our little chats."

Again the man placed the gun to Marchinko's head. He hesitated a moment or two just to watch in amusement as Marchinko suffered. When he was bored with it, he pulled the trigger.

There was another pop.

"My work here is done," he said, smirking.

With cold unconcern, he turned and walked away from the room, and as he slowly shut the door behind him, he took one last glance at the dying man on the floor.

Outside the room, he paused and peered up and down the hallway. He saw no one, heard no one. All was clear. Even if someone had heard shots and screams, this was the kind of neighborhood where no one would interfere.

Creeping along the hall and slipping down the stairs with only one almost inaudible creak, he proceeded to the street.

Back in the room, there was no more pain. No more fear. No more TJ Marchinko.

# 33

The door to TJ Marchinko's room cracked open slowly at Slick's knock. She waited a moment and listened hard. Something was wrong. The room was too quiet, like a morgue.

Except for the faint street sounds coming from outside, there wasn't even the tiniest hint of activity inside. Slick had seen death and violence far too often. She knew when their residue was hovering around.

"Laura, wait for me outside. Go across the street and keep your eyes on the windows," she whispered. "Call Sam on your cell and tell him to send a police car to meet us here. Tell him to hurry."

Laura didn't argue. She hesitated just long enough to give Slick a "be careful" look. When Laura was gone, Slick inched the door open. It creaked back on its hinges as more of the room became visible.

When she was certain no one was standing behind the door, Slick entered the room cautiously. Her basic police training kicked in as her eyes took in everything.

It was a cheap hotel room with decaying furniture and thin frayed carpeting that felt gritty. The room was basically a cube. One window. One door. No other form of access other than the one Slick was using.

The faded wallpaper was cracked and torn, and the whole place reeked of the merged smells of marijuana, cheap tobacco, cheaper liquor, and death.

Everything in the room was placidly and mutely still. Nothing screamed out there had been a struggle or violence.

Slick saw the body on the floor but first went to check the bathroom to make sure there was no one else inside. Then she circled the body and dropped down next to the earthly remains of TJ Marchinko.

The body was sprawled on the floor like a grotesque doll discarded by a fickle child. His mouth had been tightly taped shut before he was killed. Slick could make out the final agony that had contorted his face behind the tape. And his eyes, frozen in pitiful desperation, stared lifeless and unseeing at the ceiling.

Blood seeped from four bullet wounds into the dark and dirty carpet, making it darker and dirtier still.

All existence of TJ Marchinko was extinguished. There were flies buzzing around him already. Slick could only imagine how he must have suffered before being allowed to die. She gave a heavy sigh, disgusted by such a vicious murder of a man she had never met. There was nothing else she could do for him.

The bedside phone rang, loud and jarring, breaking the solemn silence, and Slick jumped, startled. Then an answering machine picked up on the fifth ring.

"Listen, Marchinko," a male voice said. "It's Whitley. Forget the diary, understand? Forget it. We don't need it." Then he hung up.

Since the fund-raiser, Slick had heard Howard Whitley

speak often enough on Kendall promo spots to recognize that he was in fact the caller.

Slick then went to the window, raised it, and looked for Laura on the crowded street below.

Laura was ducking behind the corner of a building, trying to be unseen. Slick signaled to her. When Laura saw her at the window, she started pointing frantically in the opposite direction. Slick scanned the pavement below and sent her gaze to where Laura indicated.

Her eyes locked on a man taking long rapid strides down the street, hurrying away as fast as he could. Slick's entire body stiffened.

The man she saw running away, now breaking into a fast jog, was Tom Brandeal.

# 34

On the other hand, it could be worse, Captain DeStasio decided. His mind had temporarily drifted away. He privately took stock of the past few days. During that time, he had confessed to visiting a prostitute on a regular basis, not doing his duty of reporting possible criminal behavior of a police officer to IAB, lying about it, then confessing it all to someone who may have lost all respect for him. While he watched Slick accuse Brandeal of murdering TJ Marchinko, he felt the beginnings of a headache. He was getting a lot of headaches lately.

He absentmindedly looked over at Laura. She was looking back at him with an expression that let him know she was aware he had checked out into his own thoughts for a while.

"I want you to take a polygraph," Slick demanded.

"I'm not that stupid," Brandeal said.

"We don't know that yet."

"No way. No fucking way."

"Do you have something to hide?"

"Nothing. And you don't have a thing on me."

"What did you do with the surveillance tape from the park?" Slick asked.

Brandeal said nothing.

"What are you talking about, Slick?" DeStasio asked, rubbing his head.

"Laura and I went to Echo Lake Park. They have cameras there. We were told that Detective Brandeal had taken the tape from the night Gloria's body was found."

"Brandeal? Is that true?" the captain asked.

"Yes, Captain. I took the tape and checked it. There was nothing usable on it."

Slick stepped close to Brandeal. "You erased it, didn't you?"

"I only checked it. There was nothing there."

"You son of a . . . When were you going to mention that you had it?" Slick asked, the anger in her voice rising.

"I was going to turn it in as evidence."

"Where is the tape now?" DeStasio asked.

"In my desk."

"Get it!" DeStasio barked.

"Don't bother. Whatever was there is gone now." Slick approached DeStasio. "Make him take the poly, Captain."

"Fuck you, Slick."

"Look, Brandeal, I don't like you, and I don't trust you. You're a suspect in the murder of Gloria Roxley. I just saw you running away from the scene of another murder. And now it's possible you've tampered with evidence."

"You just want to see me take the test, to tell people you made me do it."

"That's just a fringe benefit."

"I'm not taking it, because I don't like or trust you, either, Slick."

"Well, so far you're being honest."

"I don't have to take it. I'm not on trial for murder."

"Not yet," Slick said.

"Slick, you know a poly won't stand up in court," the captain reminded her.

"I know that."

"Then what are you looking for?" DeStasio's headache was kicking in big-time now.

"Maybe just a little taste of the truth." Slick sighed, exasperated. "Captain, he's a cop. He knows how the system works, how to do dirt and how to hide the dirt. If he doesn't take the poly, I'm off this case."

The captain looked at both of them.

"Take the poly, Brandeal," he said finally.

"Captain! She'll turn it into an anal probe."

"You wish," Slick muttered.

"Do I look like Katie Couric?" Brandeal yelled.

"If only," Slick sighed.

"Captain, you know she just wants to fuck with me. We all know that's what a poly is for. It's leverage."

"Look, Brandeal, she took the case like I asked her to, and now there's been another murder that involves you. If she quits now, what kind of message will that send? It looks like you're guilty. So this is how it's going to work. You're going to take the poly."

"How do I know she won't use this against me somehow?"

"Oh, then you *do* have something to hide," Slick suggested.

"Not a thing," Brandeal said firmly.

"Then what are you afraid of?" DeStasio asked.

Brandeal said nothing for several moments. "You expect me to just go along with this?" he finally asked DeStasio.

"I expect you to do as you're told. This isn't a request, Brandeal."

"When?" Brandeal asked, resigned. "I want to circle the date and put a big smiling happy face on it."

"Let me make a phone call to Ted Helyar. He's the best in the department," DeStasio said. He picked up his phone.

Slick went and sat down next to Laura while Brandeal paced the office.

They all looked at DeStasio when the call was over.

"He's available tomorrow. If you had other plans, Brandeal, now might be a good time to cancel them."

"What if I refuse?" Brandeal attempted one last stand.

"Then I will personally escort your ass to Internal Affairs," DeStasio said.

# 35

"Don't be nervous, Detective."

"Yeah, right."

"To reiterate, this is a nonadmissible polygraph."

"Yeah, yeah, yeah. Let's just get it over with."

"Is your name Thomas Brandeal?"

"Yes."

"Are you a police detective?"

"Yes."

"Is today Friday?"

"No."

"Are you now in Alabama?"

"No."

"Did you know Gloria Roxley?"

"Yes."

"Was she your informant?"

"Yes."

"Was she a prostitute?"

"Yes."

"Were you with her on the night she died?"

"I didn't kill her."

"Yes or no, Detective. Were you with Gloria Roxley on the night she died?"

"No, I was not."

"Did you ever hit her?"

"No."

"Have you ever been involved in a serious crime?"

"Oh, give me a break. I'm police. Of course I've been in-volved in serious crimes."

"Sorry. Have you ever committed a serious crime?"

"No."

"Did you erase any portion of the park surveillance tape?"

"No."

"Did you know TJ Marchinko?"

"No."

"Did you kill TJ Marchinko?"

"No."

"Okay, we're done," Ted Helyar said.

A cell phone chirped, punctuating the tense air. Everyone looked down at their belts.

"It's me," DeStasio said. "I need to take this." He excused himself and left the room to have some privacy.

Helyar took the sheets and left Slick and Brandeal alone.

They sat in the room, avoiding looking at each other, the silence between them growing heavier with each passing minute. Both of them shifted in their chairs restlessly.

Finally, after about twenty minutes, Helyar returned. "Can I see you out in the hall, Detective Slick?" he asked.

"Sure," she said. She turned to Brandeal, giving him a "gotcha now" look.

When they were out in the hall, Helyar looked around

and leaned in conspiratorially to Slick. "I can call it like you want, Detective."

"What?"

"The poly. It's inconclusive."

"So what does that mean?"

"It means you want him to pass, he'll pass. You want him to fail, he'll fail. It can go either way . . . you know, whatever you want."

Slick felt herself flushing with annoyance. "I want the truth."

"I can help you with 'the truth.' Just tell me which truth you want."

Slick looked at him in disgust. "DeStasio said you were the best in the department."

"I am. So my evaluation of his poly will read like scripture. Everyone knows this guy is no good. He's got some real stink on him."

"He might not deserve the air he breathes, but—"

"I'm just saying I'm here for you, Detective," Helyar said.

"No wonder you can't use this in court. It's bullshit. We might as well consult a phrenologist."

DeStasio walked up and joined them.

"So, how did he do?" he asked.

Helyar started to answer the question. "The test was—"

"It was inconclusive, Captain," Slick interrupted, and stormed back into the room.

Brandeal looked up. At first he was uncertain, but when he saw Slick's face, he could tell she wasn't pleased. That made him smile. He was more relieved than she'd ever know.

"A swing and a miss there, eh, Slick?" he teased.

Slick said nothing.

"Satisfied, Captain? Now can I get unhooked from this thing?"

The captain nodded and Ted Helyar removed the clips of the polygraph from Brandeal.

Slick approached Brandeal and got up close. "Marchinko called me and told me he saw you put Gloria's body in the trunk of the car and now he's dead."

"You got witnesses?" Brandeal asked sarcastically.

"Just Marchinko."

"Not anymore, you don't." Brandeal laughed.

"That gives you the perfect reason to kill him, doesn't it? If I started asking questions on the street, I wonder how many people saw you running from his room in broad daylight?"

"I wonder how many people would say they actually saw me kill TJ Marchinko or Gloria Roxley for that matter? Why is it I keep getting the feeling that you don't believe I'm innocent?"

"Maybe because you're loaded with motive and opportunity."

"The polygraph was inconclusive, Slick. Get over it."

"Everyone knows you can beat a poly, Brandeal."

"Your case on me is weak, Slick. You're just gonna have to deal with how much you hate me. I'll be here through the rest of your bullshit, because I'm not going anywhere."

"Until this case is over, neither am I."

Brandeal started for the door. DeStasio stepped in front of him. "Hand over your gun and your shield, Brandeal," the captain said.

"What the hell for?"

"The test was inconclusive. That doesn't clear you, does it?"

Brandeal stared at him angrily.

The captain didn't back down. "It's up to you how this goes," DeStasio said. It was subtle, but there was a threat.

Brandeal gave up his gun and badge, then he turned and almost took the door off its hinges on the way out.

"Catch you later, Brandeal," Slick called after him as he left.

"Well, now what?" DeStasio asked when they were alone.

"Captain, I know Brandeal is involved in this somehow."

The captain looked at her closely. Slick wondered if he doubted her.

"Okay, Slick. You work the case your way. I've some business to attend to."

Just beyond the office door, as DeStasio left, Slick could see Ted Helyar speaking with Sam. She started to approach, but when she saw Paula join them, she thought it best to stay away. After the fight they had had, she couldn't face Paula with nothing substantial to pin on Brandeal.

She left through another door, feeling ashamed of herself for avoiding two of her best friends.

# 36

The sound of the doorbell didn't merely awaken Jerry Jankowski; it snapped him into an upright position in his sweat-soaked bed, his underwear damp and clinging. He couldn't remember when he had finally drifted off to sleep. He was groggy and disoriented.

Most of the night had been spent adjusting and punching his pillow. He had tossed and turned so much the sheets had come undone from the bed.

Shading his eyes now from the sunlight that streamed into this borrowed apartment, he glanced at the clock on the dresser. It was after two in the afternoon.

The sound of the buzzer beckoned again.

At first Jerry thought he could ignore it. He pulled the covers up to his shoulders, put a pillow over his head, and tried to force himself to ignore it. For several seconds he succeeded.

But when the buzzer sounded again, he knew he had no choice. It would continue until he answered the door. He couldn't dismiss it any more than he could dismiss the faint nervousness in his stomach.

He violently kicked off the covers, got to his feet, and slipped into a robe. He caught a glimpse of himself in the bedroom mirror. The man staring back at him was a stranger. The past few weeks had taken their toll. He'd had never been hunk-handsome, but the good looks he did have were in jeopardy. Jerry did not like seeing proof of it in this unflattering mirror. He walked with hesitant steps through the apartment.

Crossing directly to the door, he looked through the peephole, knowing who it was before he looked but looking anyway. His hand reached slowly for the doorknob, but he stopped short. His life was about to change dramatically. He toyed with the idea that he could forestall what was coming just by refusing to open the door and start the ball rolling. But he made the deal. He had to go through with it.

The bell vibrated again in its irritating impersonal manner. Jerry opened the door.

Howard Whitely stood in the doorway. "It took you long enough to answer the door. I was getting a little worried."

"Sorry, I was asleep."

"I'm not the kind of man who likes to be kept waiting."

"It won't happen again."

"No, it won't," Whitley said, then he broke into a big smile. "Well, aren't you going to ask me in?"

"Like I have a choice."

Whitely smiled. "It's good to see you. You're looking good."

Jerry extended his hand to shake. Whitely did the same, but when Whitely shook it, Jerry felt a strange vibration and he jerked away rapidly.

Howard stepped into the apartment and surveyed it with an approving eye.

"This is nice," he said, looking around. "You have everything you need—cable TV, the Internet, a well-stocked bar. Very nice."

Jerry shrugged. "I just can't talk to anyone. I feel like a recluse."

"Don't worry. This won't last much longer," Whitley assured him.

"Really?" Jerry sounded only half relieved.

"Really. We just didn't want you to be recognized before you were needed. Now you're needed."

"What?"

Whitley sank into the couch. "We've had to push up the schedule on this thing."

"What do you mean?"

"You have an interview in one hour."

Jerry panicked. "I'm not ready. No way."

"Don't get excited. I've written down everything you need to say. You'll do fine."

"I'm not ready."

"You'll be ready. Go shower and dress. I've got a car waiting for you outside. We can go over everything on the ride to the studio."

"I'm afraid I'll screw this up."

"Don't worry, just tell the truth like you told it to me. Do exactly as I say, and there won't be any screwups."

"I don't know. People . . . his family . . . they're going to get hurt."

"Probably," Whitley said coldly.

"The timing of this . . . He'll be ruined for a long time."

"That's the idea."

"Can't we call him? Give him some warning?"

"No. We need him to look bad. We need a scandal. We need it now."

Jerry stood silently, scared. It was becoming real too fast.

"Look, we have a deal. You agreed to this for fifty grand. Here's half of it." Whitley threw the money at Jerry. The bundle landed at his feet. "Now you can get started on . . . your project."

A sense of helplessness passed through Jerry as he looked at the money on the floor. He needed it badly. Slowly he bent down and picked it up.

Howard Whitley was pleased. "When the interview is over, you'll get the rest."

"Then what?"

"Then my car will take you anywhere you want to go. You can leave and start your life over. You won't have to be available for any further comment when the shit hits the fan."

## This Is Action News 10 in New Jersey . . . All of New Jersey All of the Time

"Hello, I'm Michelle Tevotino. Thanks for joining us. We have breaking news. In an exclusive interview with a former male prostitute, Action News 10 in New Jersey has learned that Family Values Conservative Republican Pete Moreno was sexually involved with the male prostitute for years.

"Joining us now is Jerry Jankowski. Why did you feel you had to come forward now, Jerry?"

"I've agonized over this for a long time before I came forward. I mean, Pete has a family. I don't want to hurt them. And I genuinely care about Pete. But, finally, I felt I had to. The legislature in New Jersey is considering gay marriage or civil unions and the U.S. Congress regularly tries to get an amendment banning gay marriage. Pete would have a say in that. And it's just so hypocritical."

"How long was your relationship with Pete Moreno?"

"Three years."

"What you are looking at now on your screen is old file footage of Pete Moreno carrying a sign saying 'God Hates Fags' at a family values rally."

" 'I will never vote to endorse gay unions, because it's in the Bible that it's wrong and that is the word of God. So we don't need to debate the issue in a general assembly.' "

"This just in, our camera crew is outside the Moreno home. We go live to them, where Pete Moreno is making a statement."

" 'These allegations are completely false. I stand for

integrity and decency. I love my wife, football, and the flag. This is a last-minute attempt to smear my good name before the election.'"

"Your comments, Jerry?"

"I have names, dates, and birthmarks. I have further proof of other men Pete Moreno has been with. E-mails, letters, gay Web sites, and gay dating services. I can make this proof available at any time."

"Anything else you'd like to say, Jerry?"

"If you're going to be an in-the-closet Republican, be better at it."

# 37

Jerry Jankowski unlocked the door of the apartment he had secretly been held in and then slammed it behind him. He was out of breath after running up the stairs.

He was free now. The unpleasantness was behind him. He told his story, got paid, and now it was time to get on with his life.

With nothing more to worry about, he went to the refrigerator and took out the bottle of wine he had saved for this night. He consumed about two-thirds of it and still didn't feel relieved. He couldn't get the thought of Pete Moreno out of his mind. He couldn't shake off his feelings of guilt.

He tried to tell himself it wasn't his fault. He didn't pursue Moreno and make him gay. He hadn't forced the guy to cheat on his wife and lie to his family.

*The truth shall set you free,* Jerry thought. But the sense of dread he felt wasn't at all like being set free. What if he was damned for telling the truth?

Jerry put down the package he had been carrying. It contained the rest of his money. His pieces of silver, he thought. Jerry wanted to open the package and look at it right now,

but he was disciplined. He'd open the package later and let all
the green pour over him.

He looked around the apartment. It depressed him, but he
wouldn't be here much longer. Now he had what he needed:
fifty thousand in cash. He could leave right away. He was
tired of New Jersey. Time to move on. Time to start fresh.

Jerry turned on the television.

> . . . *Republican Pete Moreno, running for U.S. senator from
> New Jersey, is seen here surrounded by reporters after being accused of
> involvement with a male prostitute* . . .

Jerry changed the channel.

> . . . *outed by a gay male prostitute, senatorial hopeful Pete
> Moreno* . . .

Jerry turned off the television.

He took off all his clothes, grabbed the bottle of wine,
and walked into the bathroom to take a much needed bath.
In this apartment building, only one bathroom in each apartment had a tub. The others had a shower stall. Jerry hadn't felt
right in a shower in a while.

He walked to the tub and turned on the water, carefully
adjusting the dials to produce a temperature that was just right.
Jerry was going to lounge in the tub for at least an hour, he
promised himself, because a bath ought to be a leisurely experience, relaxing and sensual. It was just what he needed.

He could get clean and focused and decide what he was
going to do next. He was sorry, though, that he didn't have
anything bubbly to put in the water as he soaked. No matter.
He took another chug from the wine bottle.

When the depth and the temperature of the water pleased him, he dimmed the light, stepped into the tub, and sat down.

Oh, it felt so good. Then, closing his eyes, he slid lower until only his head was above the water. It felt like a sweet caress. The only sound in the room was his own breathing.

Then a familiar voice whispered, "Hello, Jerry."

Jerry's eyes shot open and he started, gasping for air, nearly choking on the breaths he took in.

"We need to talk," the man said calmly. He leaned over the tub, then reached out a hand that went under the water. Jerry shrank from it and tried to scream, but with all the water he took in, it came out only a gurgle.

"Don't be afraid, Jerry. This won't take long." The man's hand was searching along the bottom of the tub.

"Ah, yes. There it is." The man smiled and pulled the plug on Jerry.

Scared and shivering, Jerry could only watch as the water drained away, exposing his nakedness, exposing his fear.

# 38

"Thank you for taking the time to meet with us," Slick said as she and Laura entered Kendall's private office at his campaign headquarters.

"Not at all," Kendall said. "Have you come to give me a contribution, Ms. Charles?" he joked.

"I wish our reasons were so simple," Laura said.

"Sounds serious. Before we start, can I offer you both a bottled water? I don't drink coffee or tea."

"No, thank you," they said.

"Okay, then, how can I help you?"

"When I met you at the fund-raiser the other night, we talked about an investigation I'm currently involved in," Slick said.

"Yes, the one involving the police officer."

"That's right. Did you know he's a suspect in the murder of a prostitute?"

"No, I didn't."

"Her street name was Paradise. Her real name was Gloria Roxley."

Kendall's face went white. "Oh, my God. She's been murdered?"

"Yes, and her friend TJ Marchinko has also been murdered."

"You think this has something to do with the diary?"

"That's what I'm trying to find out."

"I have no reason to kill Gloria or anyone else."

"Really? There's pretty damaging information in the diary about you. Information you wouldn't want to come out to your family, and certainly not in the middle of a campaign. TJ Marchinko mentioned your name. He was afraid. Now he's dead."

"Look, Detective, my wife knows all about my relationship with Gloria."

Slick and Laura both looked startled.

"Now isn't that interesting. Wouldn't that give her a motive to want to see Gloria dead?" Slick asked.

"No."

"No? You're paying for sex with another woman, and your wife wouldn't feel some hostility about that?"

"Apparently you haven't read the diary very closely, Detective. Most of the time I was with Gloria, my wife was there, too."

Laura coughed and suddenly had trouble breathing. "I'll take that bottle of water now," she said.

Kendall took one from the cooler by his desk and handed it to Laura. "Don't look so shocked, Ms. Charles. A lot of the elite found their way into Gloria's diary. Please feel free to question my wife if you like."

Neither Slick nor Laura could understand how he could discuss his sex life so blithely.

"Even if that's true, what about your campaign?" Slick asked.

"Well, Howard and I did have a few arguments about it. Quite a few loud arguments, in fact. We talked about trying to get it back, but then I told him to forget about it. He thought I was foolish to trust that the diary would remain undisclosed, but I was emphatic, so that was the end of it as far as I was concerned."

"Why were you so positive the diary wouldn't become public knowledge?" Laura asked.

"Because I know Pete Moreno. We are on different sides of the issues, but he is a man of his word. When your associate, Ms. O'Hare, approached Pete, he called me. You see, I've known for years that Pete was gay. We agreed that I wouldn't bring up his personal life in the campaign, and he wouldn't bring up mine. That's why neither of us took Ms. O'Hare up on her offer.

"And your reputation precedes you, Ms. Charles. You're not the type to go around blackmailing people. You're too fond of your charity not to be discreet about the private lives of your contributors. So you see, it was really good for me and Pete that the diary wound up with you. There was no reason for me to kill anyone."

"If you and Moreno had this arrangement, then why was Jerry Jankowski on television yesterday outing Moreno?" Slick asked.

For the first time, Kendall seemed upset. "That was Howard Whitley's doing. Apparently, I can trust my opponent more than I can trust my campaign manager. I came in today to see what kind of damage control I could do, issue some kind of statement without losing votes."

They were all alarmed by the sudden pummeling on Kendall's office door.

"Goddamn you!" Pete Moreno came charging in.

Kendall jumped up from behind his desk and went to Moreno, trying to placate him. "Pete," he said, "believe me, I had nothing to do with it."

"You're lying, you rotten fuck!" Moreno yelled. "We had a deal."

"Pete, it was Howard Whitley, I swear. He put Jankowski up to it. I went to see Jankowski."

"You know for sure that Whitley was behind Jankowski going to the press?" Slick asked.

"Yes." Kendall sighed. "I found him at the apartment I keep. Whitley had him holed up there. Jankowski confessed everything. Whitley gave him fifty thousand dollars."

Slick leaned into Kendall, watching him very closely. "Just how did you get him to confess?"

"He was in the bathtub . . . naked. He was scared. I scared him. That's all. I didn't hurt him."

Moreno pounded his fist on Kendall's desk. "What are you going to do about it?" he demanded.

"Pete, we're in the middle of a campaign," Kendall stammered. "I can't fire Whitley now. How would that look? But as soon as it's over, Whitley's out, I swear."

"You're still worried about the campaign? I'm ruined!" Moreno exploded.

"Let me walk out with you and we'll discuss it." Kendall crossed to him.

"Get the fuck out of my way," Moreno said. Like an angry bull, he marched back out the way he had come in, with Kendall running behind him.

# 39

The phone began to ring just as Sheleeta was applying another coat of nail polish to her toes and watching *The Birdcage* on cable. Lady D was busy preparing dinner.

Sheleeta put down the polish brush, picked up the remote, and turned up the volume to drown out the sound of the clanging pots and pans and the ringing phone.

"You want to answer that?" Lady shouted from the kitchen.

"I can't. I'm indisposed."

"You're doing your toenails."

"And they haven't dried yet."

There was a loud crash from the kitchen.

"The last time you were off that couch of your own volition, Sheleeta, was when it was on fire," Lady said angrily as she picked up the kitchen phone.

Sheleeta laughed gleefully and shouted, "Girl, you got to come in here. This is your favorite part. Gene Hackman in a wig! Can you imagine?"

Lady finished the call, then entered the living room looking very serious. She picked up the remote and turned off the television.

Sheleeta started to protest, but when she saw the look on Lady's face, she shut her mouth. The movie was almost over, anyway.

"Our girl Slick needs our help," Lady said.

"Anything for her. What is it?"

"She needs us to put eyes on this cop Brandeal. She needs us to say that it was him who grabbed Paradise on Halsey Street and that we can positively identify him."

"But we didn't see a thing."

"I know. She's sure it's him but can't get a break on the case. I said we'd do it, go down to the police station and give them our statements."

Sheleeta looked hesitant.

"You think I should have refused," Lady asked.

"No. It's nice to be needed. It's for Slick and for Paradise. When do we go?"

"As soon as possible. First thing in the morning. Okay?"

Sheleeta nodded enthusiastically and pointed at the TV screen.

Lady sighed but turned the television back on and returned to the kitchen.

The movie was just ending.

*"We are family. I got all my sisters with me."*

# 40

Lady Dijonnaise leaned toward the full-length mirror and brushed her wig. It was a luxurious sensuous brushing of the long black hair. Across the room, Sheleeta positioned her own wig, which was short and blond, and arranged the elfish mop of curls.

Their hair in place, they both applied makeup generously. Lady fringed her eyes with deep blue mascara and Sheleeta used black. Each painted her lips a rosy red and smiled tightly to smooth the lipstick.

They finished dressing, then looked in their mirrors together, admiring each other. Their red dresses hugged their opulent hips, accentuating their well-used bodies. They were proud of how they looked. They checked each other for flaws and found none.

"Fashionistas," they said in unison.

"You're beautiful."

"So are you."

"Do you think these heels are too high?" Sheleeta wondered.

"Just high enough. This is not work. I'd say this is more business casual."

"Are you sure?"

"Would I lead you wrong, little sister?"

Sheleeta smiled. If she had dimples, she would have flashed them.

"It's a beautiful day; let's walk to the police station," Lady suggested.

"Girl, I can't remember walking voluntarily to the police station," Sheleeta commented.

"Ain't that the truth. But this is for a good cause."

"I wouldn't do this for anyone but Slick."

"Okay, here we go. Remember your manners, Sheleeta."

"Don't use that hectoring tone with me. Of course I'll remember my manners."

They started down the stairs, which creaked from the collective weight, opened the door, and stepped out into the bright morning light.

# 41

"Captain?"

"Yes?"

"There are two witnesses here to give statements on the Gloria Roxley murder."

The officer was smiling broadly.

"So why are you bothering me? Take their statements."

"They say they can positively identify the murderer, and they said they'd speak only to you."

DeStasio looked at his watch. He had no pressing appointments. He hadn't taken a statement in a long time, but he was willing to do anything to solve this case.

"Okay, show them in," he said.

The officer glanced over his shoulder. He did not stop smiling. "He'll see you now . . . ladies."

The captain stood up from his desk and buttoned his jacket.

Lady Dijionnaise and Sheleeta Buffet breezed into his office.

DeStasio looked up and saw the largest transvestites he had ever seen. With them standing next to each other, the captain was certain they had their own zip code. They towered over him. And they were twins.

He shot a look at the officer, who backed out of the office, trying to hide a grin, and closed the door. The hallway beyond DeStasio's office erupted in laughter.

DeStasio regained his composure and forced an awkward smile. "Please come in," he said.

They entered as daintily as they could. "Are you the gentleman we're supposed to see about the murder of Paradise? We want to get this right. We would hate to repeat this to someone else. We abhor repetition."

"We abhor repetition," the twin repeated.

"Yes, I'm Captain DeStasio."

"Captain DeStasio, so good of you to see us. Perhaps we were not properly introduced. I'm Lady Dijionnaise, and this is my sister, Sheleeta Buffet."

They extended their meaty hands palms down as if to be kissed, but the captain pretended not to see that and motioned for them to sit down.

They squeezed themselves as best they could into the chairs in front of his desk.

"First, may we start off by saying that we have been brought here many times for our work as sex providers, and your officers have always treated us with courtesy and respect. Especially former officer Cassandra Slick."

"I'm glad to hear that. Please go on with your story. I'm going to take notes. Do you mind?"

"Not at all," Lady said.

"Is it true that the police have no clues?" Sheleeta asked.

"That's what the newspapers are saying, but it's not entirely true."

"Well, we know that Officer Tom Brandeal manhandled her—Paradise—and snatched her off Halsey Street. We saw him," Lady said.

"Where were you?"

"We were across the street at a KFC taking a little snack break."

"We had a bucket of Original Recipe, corn on the cob, mac and cheese, biscuits, and those wonderful little bucket parfaits," said Sheleeta.

"It has tables facing the windows that overlook Halsey Street," Lady explained.

"What time was this?"

"About ten at night."

"And you can positively identify Brandeal?"

"Yes," Lady said.

"You'll testify to that?"

"Certainly. That's the zing we bring to the table," Sheleeta said.

"Why are you coming forward now?"

"Well, at first we thought they were just having a little spat, you know. Sometimes things get a little rough on the street. But nothing like this."

"How did you know Brandeal?"

"All the workers knew that Paradise was working for him as his snitch. He was often on Halsey Street getting information, but he was a bad cop; everyone knew that," Lady said.

"Personally, I think someone peed in his gene pool," Sheleeta added.

"Had you ever seen him mistreat her before?"

Lady and Sheleeta exchanged a look.

"Well, no," they said in unison.

The captain wrote up their statements and took their address and phone number. Then he looked up and thanked them for coming in.

When they hesitated looking at him, he understood what they wanted.

"Let me get the door for you."

"If you would be so kind," Lady said.

# 42

*"Cassie! Cassie! Let's play hide-and-seek. You're it."*

*Cassie went to the closest tree in the park and started counting to ten.*

*She looked for Gloria everywhere. It was getting dark, and she still couldn't find her. She started to get scared.*

*"Gloria! Gloria! Come out! Where are you? I can't find you!"*

Slick's phone started to ring. It was late. Laura was asleep beside her, and Garbo was curled up on the edge of the bed.

She fumbled for the lamp beside the bed. She was still fuzzy from her dream, but she managed to say, "Hello."

"We're sorry to call so late. We're just getting off work. We just had to alert you and give you the good news."

"Lady? Sheleeta?"

"Yes, girlfriend, your case will be resolved."

"What do you mean?"

"Brandeal is going away for killing Paradise," Lady said.

Slick was wide awake now. Her eyes flew open.

"I have no idea what you're talking about."

"Well, we got the call that you needed some help in solving the Paradise murder case, so we helped."

"What did you do?"

"We went to police headquarters first thing this morning and gave statements that we saw Brandeal take Paradise from Halsey Street."

"But you told me you didn't see him."

"We didn't, but we wanted to help you."

"Who did you talk to?"

"A Captain DeStasio."

"And he believed you?"

"Of course he believed me," Lady said, somewhat offended. "I have a gift for fiction. I always wanted to be an actress."

"I always wanted to be a chanteuse," Sheleeta said in the background.

"We wanted to do something to help, something to assuage our deep sense of guilt and loss."

"Was DeStasio the only person you talked to?"

"Yes. He's a very kind man."

"Lady, I don't understand. What makes you think I would want you to give false statements?"

"We got a call that you needed help with the case."

"Who called you and said I needed help?"

"Officer Rafferty. Paula Rafferty."

# 43

"What the hell were you thinking, Paula?" Slick demanded. She was so angry she paid no attention to the man seated at Paula's desk. "I can't believe you interfered in my investigation. I know you're angry with me, but soliciting false statements from Lady and Sheleeta? What the hell is wrong with you?"

She stopped in mid-rant when Paula held up a picture. Slick's jaw dropped.

"Where'd you get this?" she asked.

Paula indicated the man at her desk.

"Who are you?" Slick asked.

"I'm Hamilton Baker."

"How well do you know Detective Rafferty?"

"We've never met. This is our first meeting."

"Who requested this meeting?"

"I came here on my own."

"How'd you get this picture?"

"I had been in Echo Lake Park walking my dog. I saw the man in the cowboy hat. I took his picture with my cell phone."

"Why?"

"My dog had come close to attacking him. I took the picture to make sure he was all right and wouldn't try to sue me later. See, I was in the middle of the Shaw murder case."

"Yes. I recognize you now."

"Then I remembered a car had passed me on the path. I didn't think there was a possible connection to the murder until later."

"The car passed you right before you saw this man?"

"Yes. It was a matter of only a few minutes."

"Do you mind if I get back to my interview, Slick?" Paula asked.

Slick shook her head no, and Paula took the formal statement from Hamilton Baker.

Slick barely heard them talking. Her eyes were still riveted on the picture. It was Tom Brandeal. Definitely.

# 44

Frank DeStasio drove through the droning soggy night. He hated driving in the rain. The headlights picked up the water flooding the streets. The wipers, on high, couldn't keep up with the rain pelting the windshield.

He parked in his spot and turned his coat collar up and walked to the jail.

"Captain," the sergeant on duty said as DeStasio passed. DeStasio nodded in acknowledgment.

He gave his gun to the guard on duty and entered the cell.

He looked at the drunk on the floor in disgust and sat down on the cot.

Tom Brandeal awoke abruptly out of an alcohol-sodden sleep. He was on a cold concrete floor. He rolled his head and tried to lift it. It wasn't easy, so he stopped trying. His brain felt too big for his skull.

The next thing he was aware of was the sour odor of his own body. His bladder was full, and his tongue tasted like rat piss, a sour reminder of last night's excess.

How could scotch taste so smooth going down and hours later taste like the fumes of liquid crap? As if to answer his own question, he ran his dry tongue around his mouth and picked up the salty taste of blood.

He ran his hand over his face and felt caked vomit. There was a tender place on his forehead, the size of a peach.

A voice came out of the quiet. "Jesus, you stink."

"Fuck you," Brandeal said, not recognizing the voice.

Excellent. Signs of life, DeStasio thought. "How's the hangover? Painful, I hope," DeStasio said.

"It's not so bad," Brandeal lied.

"Then I guarantee this will be."

Suddenly there was a powerful kick to his ribs.

Brandeal gasped in pain as more blood ran into his mouth.

"This is why I usually wake up alone," he managed to say. "I always seem to have pissed off anyone who's with me."

"You're lucky I had to leave my piece outside the door."

"See what I mean? That's downright hostile."

Brandeal fell silent, and DeStasio thought he was drifting back into drunken sleep or at least semiconsciousness.

"Wake up, you piece of shit."

"Where am I?"

"You're in the city drunk tank."

"What the hell am I doing here?"

"I had you picked up."

"Why?"

"You got drunk in a bar and started acting up. There was a fight. The bartender knew you were a cop, so he called the station. He didn't want any trouble, didn't want you driving home in your condition. He was right. You blew a two-point-oh."

"How long have I been here?"

"About three hours." DeStasio kicked him again.

"Ow! What the hell is wrong with you?"

"You killed her, you son of a bitch. You killed her."

Vague and dreamy pieces of the previous night floated into Brandeal's mind, but he couldn't arrange them in a way that made sense. He badly needed aspirin. About twenty should do it.

"A lot of people don't like you and wouldn't miss you if you were dead."

"Are you going to be the one to do it? Here and now?"

"Don't tempt me. It would be justifiable homicide."

"I don't care what you do with me."

DeStasio bent down and grabbed Brandeal by the collar and pulled him to his feet, as if he weighed next to nothing.

"I didn't kill her."

"You lying sack of shit. I've got two eyewitnesses who say you were the one who grabbed her off Halsey Street." DeStasio raised his fist and was about to punch him.

"Please don't. I didn't kill her."

"You're going to have to do better than that. You saying it over and over doesn't convince me. I've lost what little faith I had in you, given recent events."

"I think I'm going to be sick."

DeStasio studied his face. He seemed to have aged ten years in the past few weeks. It was a declining graph of drinking and lack of sleep. There were basset hound bags under each eye.

"Why are you trying to drink yourself to death?"

"I'm still alive, aren't I?"

"What are you looking for in the bottle?"

"When I find it, I'll let you know."

"If you're looking for sympathy, you're not going to get it."

"Did I mention I'm going to be sick?"

The captain's cell phone rang. He let go of Brandeal, and he slumped to the floor.

He answered the phone and listened closely.

"I'm with Brandeal now. We'll meet you in my office."

He clicked off, then returned his attention to Brandeal. "That was Slick. She says she wants to meet with us at the office."

"I guess that will bring this little dance we've been doing to an end."

"That's right. You're running out of time, Brandeal. Anything you want to tell me?"

"So, first you want to kill me, and now you're my priest, waiting to hear my confession. I'm deeply touched, but you should worry about yourself."

"What have you got to say, Brandeal?" DeStasio shook him.

"Just this."

Brandeal threw up and ruined DeStasio's suit. Then he passed out.

"Son of a bitch," DeStasio muttered. He had just bought the suit.

## This Is News 10 in New Jersey . . . All of
## New Jersey All of the Time

"It's eleven P.M. and the polls have closed. News 10 in New Jersey is predicting that Clinton Kendall will win by a large margin over his Republican challenger and be elected as U.S. senator from New Jersey. Once again, New Jersey voters overturned a proposed bond issue that would have set aside monies for the redevelopment of sections of Newark, Trenton, and Camden.

"New Jersey is blamed for a natural gas-like odor that hung over much of Manhattan and parts of New Jersey this afternoon. There were reports that the odious stink was detected as far away as Pennsylvania and Delaware. Emergency operators were bombarded with calls demanding to know the source of the smell.

"Both the NYC mayor and New Jersey governor assured their citizens that there was no indication that the air was unsafe and no indication of a terrorist plot. As a precaution, however, some commuter trains running between New Jersey and Manhattan were suspended for about two hours. A few city schools were briefly evacuated, and city dwellers were advised to keep their windows closed. Fifteen people from Manhattan's Chelsea section were taken to hospitals with minor complaints from breathing irritation.

"'The smell was stinky, toxic. I got dizzy from it,'" one sufferer was quoted as saying. New Jersey is no stranger to odd smells.

"And some 'small-time crooks' have been apprehended in Edison. Chief of police, Sarjeet Patel, reported that the gang has confessed to several break-ins over the past few months. All gang members are between eighteen and twenty-three years and diminutive. The chief did not say if they were dwarfs or just small.

"Well, that's law and odor here in the Garden State."

# 45

Slick and Laura were waiting in DeStasio's office when the captain entered with a very drunk Tom Brandeal in tow. DeStasio parked him on the sofa, then turned his attention to Slick. "What have you got?" the captain asked.

"Just a minute please, Captain." DeStasio watched as Slick approached Brandeal with something in her hand. "Does this look familiar to you, Brandeal?" Slick asked. She held the picture up to his face, but he turned away and said nothing.

"This is a picture taken of you in Echo Lake Park. The picture was taken by a jogger who thought his dog bit you." She then passed the picture to DeStasio, who looked at it closely.

"This is Brandeal at the park, wearing the cowboy hat the motel clerk described," he said.

"Yes, sir, it's Brandeal. I'm guessing he had just disposed of the car Gloria's body was found in," Slick answered.

"So, he did kill her?" The anger in DeStasio's voice was apparent to everyone.

Slick watched and waited for Brandeal to start proclaiming his innocence as usual, but he said nothing. Instead, he looked at the floor and seemed resigned to his guilty fate.

"No, Captain," Slick said. "Brandeal didn't kill Gloria."

The captain looked up from the photo, startled.

Slick continued. "Brandeal was trying to help Gloria leave town and begin her new life. Gloria asked Brandeal to help stage her 'death.' With her full cooperation, he staged her death by making her disappear from Halsey Street, making sure she would be remembered by the clerk on duty at the motel, the two of them acting drunk, him wearing the cowboy hat so the man with Paradise would be remembered.

"Once they got into the motel room, Brandeal wrapped Gloria in a blanket, and he put the blanket in the trunk so the police would find DNA evidence there," Slick explained.

"But there was so much blood found at the motel," the captain said.

"Meldrick, the ME, said that the body had not lost much blood," Slick said.

They all looked at Brandeal.

"I got a supply of blood to leave at the motel to make it look like a murder," he said slowly, without looking at anyone.

"It was all faked," Slick said. "Besides, Gloria's exclusive clientele would never have taken her to such a sleazy motel. After Gloria got out of the trunk, Brandeal drove the car and submerged it in the shallow water of Echo Lake. Brandeal wanted the police to have no trouble finding the car. He knew they would probably conclude that she was the victim of a murder whose body was not recovered.

"Gloria was very much alive the last time Brandeal saw her. After she and Brandeal did their charade at the motel, she went to meet her friend Marchinko to start her new life. What she did not know was that someone had convinced

Marchinko to betray her. She had told him about Brandeal's plan to stage her death. This worked out perfectly for the man who killed her.

"Marchinko thought that Gloria would keep the journal and bring it with her, but at the last minute, she decided she did not want that hanging over her head in her new life. She felt they would both be safer without it. Gloria told Marchinko she put the journal in the mail to me, at Laura's foundation. She didn't know where we lived, but she did have the address for the foundation. When Marchinko found out that she did not have the journal with her, he knew the person who had hired him to get it would not like this loose end. And he was right—that man killed her and told Marchinko to put her body in the trunk of the car that was still in the lake, making it look like Brandeal had really killed her after all. And he told Marchinko to get the diary.

"Mrs. Roxley knew that Gloria was planning to leave with Marchinko, so when he asked her for my cell phone number, telling her he may have some information on Gloria's death, she didn't think twice about giving it to him. But before he could get it, Marchinko was killed. Who killed Marchinko? The same man who killed Gloria.

"At first I thought it was Brandeal when I saw him running from the apartment. But I think he just went there to talk with him. I think that's why Brandeal got the park tape; he wanted to see what else was on the tape. When he saw himself, he erased that part, but then he saw Marchinko put the body in the trunk later that night. When Marchinko was killed, he erased all of it, because it would look like he had the greatest motive to kill him."

"So who killed Gloria and Marchinko?" the captain asked.

"Howard Whitley," Slick said.

"You said Whitley called when you found Marchinko's body," Laura said.

"That was just to give himself an alibi if he ever needed it. He knew Marchinko was dead when he called," Slick explained. "The one thing Gloria, Marchinko, and Jerry Jankowski all had in common was that they were all prostitutes who had been represented by Whitley when he was a lawyer. He reminded me of that when he told me I had arrested so many of his clients."

"You don't think Kendall had anything to do with all this, do you? After all, his name was in the diary," DeStasio said.

"Kendall wasn't concerned about that information leaking out, since he knew I had the diary and wouldn't say anything—the information it contained would be as damaging to me and my foundation as it would be to his campaign," Laura said.

"No, I think Whitley acted alone," Slick said. "Kendall may have not been concerned about the journal, but Whitley was. As campaign manager, he wanted the journal, just in case he needed leverage to get Kendall elected or needed favors after Kendall was elected. Whitely thought Kendall might be grateful one day that he had the foresight to get it. And if nothing else, he could use the information against Kendall if he ever needed to. Plus, Whitley acted behind Kendall's back in getting Jerry Jankowski to out Pete Moreno. Whitley was doing everything he could to cement his 'power behind the throne' status."

DeStasio took a moment to let it all sink in. "Well, Brandeal," he said finally, "I guess you are innocent. Do you have anything to say?"

"Can I go now?"

DeStasio looked at him with disgust. "Get out of here."

When Brandeal had left, the captain said, "Brandeal might be ungrateful for your hard work, but I'm not. Soon I'll be sending a couple officers to question Mr. Howard Whitley."

"Thank you," Slick said.

Slick and Laura shook hands with DeStasio and left.

# 46

*RING RING RING RING RING RING RING RING*

Pete Moreno sat at his large desk in shadows. He was in his home office with its high ceiling and stone hearth fireplace. For a very busy man, his desk was strikingly uncluttered. On it were two photographs in identical silver frames, one on the left side and one on the right. One picture was of his wife, Candace, waving from the bow of their sailboat somewhere on the Jersey Shore; the other was a picture of their two children. There was a blotter and a silver cigarette case.

He took a cigarette from the silver case and lit it. He was trying to quit, but life was short and experimenting with new ideas could be perilous.

He stared stupidly at the words in front of him. He had continued to stare at them for hours after reading them through. Perhaps another hour had passed, maybe three. He could not say when night had fallen.

The cigarette that dangled from his mouth dropped ash on the expensive leather blotter on his desk. At first he didn't notice. He savagely crumpled the messages and the printed-out e-mails and flung them violently into the fire. The cigarette fell away and burned a hole in the blotter. He quickly wiped away the ash and examined the damage.

"If she sees this, she'll kill me," he said aloud. He put some saliva on his finger and tried to mend it. It was a few seconds before he remembered it wasn't necessary anymore. He picked up the remains of the cigarette, took a long drag, and went into a long coughing jag.

"They're right. These things will kill you." Then he put the cigarette out.

In the background, phones were ringing. They hadn't stopped ringing since the gay thing had appeared about him online and and in the papers.

Moreno screamed for the phones to stop ringing, but they didn't. He lost the election and all his future political ambitions, and he was about to lose his family, too.

Candace had taken the children to her parents' home and had already begun divorce proceedings.

Pete guessed that somehow his wife had known all along that he was gay. They had never openly discussed it, of course, but there had been clues; Pete was certain. She probably had some dim recognition of it, subliminal though it may have been, and decided to tolerate it.

As long as Pete had his secret under control, control meant happiness and conformity meant bliss. Now that Pete's gayness was all over the news, Candace Moreno had found their life together distinctly intolerable.

Pete got up from his desk and walked over to the fireplace. His legs felt weak and watery. He stood there, rigidly staring into the flames. He was an elegant man who had served his community as best he could. He had always wanted to be a politician, a leader.

But that dream occurred in a previous life, lived by another version of himself. And now that dream was going up in flames, like the papers he had flung inside it.

Now the nightmare started. He had a sense of unreality. He held up his hand and studied it. It seemed disconnected from him. Even his body had abandoned him. A tiredness was deep inside him, a leaden-muscled nerve-frayed fatigue. He was unaware of time, just seemed to be floating alone, lost and insignificant. Dead.

Then a curious gleam filled his eyes. He had nothing to lose anymore. Nothing to hide and nothing to protect. Nothing to live for. He had always known that his secret might come out. His mind was in torment now, and the phones kept ringing in the background.

He thought momentarily of throwing himself on the flames. He stepped closer and closer, leaning in, the heat licking at him. He tried to imagine what the headlines would be then: FAILED CANDIDATE IN GAY SCANDAL THROWS HIMSELF INTO THE FIRE, on the front page of every newspaper in the country.

Pete Moreno tried but couldn't do it. It would take too long, and the pain may cause him to instinctively retreat. He'd still be alive, just mutilated.

Gradually his pose slackened, and he backed away from the flames.

### *RING RING RING RING RING RING RING RING*

"Would somebody please answer the phones?" he whispered. When he was a candidate, his every wish was attended to. But he was alone now, deserted by everyone, and the phones continued to ring. Of course, he could have gone downstairs and ripped the phones out of the wall, but if he left the sanctuary of his study, there'd be a news reporter waiting at the window to snap his picture. And he couldn't take that chance.

There was a gun he kept in his desk for protection. He walked to his desk, sat down, and opened the drawer where he hid the weapon. He took it out now and looked at it closely. It wasn't loaded, so he did that now. He sat up straight, took a deep breath, then placed the barrel of the gun against his temple. Sweat gathered on his forehead. His fingers stiffened.

### *RING RING RING RING RING RING RING*

Moreno slumped forward in his chair and started groaning. "Will someone please answer the fucking phone? I'm trying to commit suicide here."

No one answered it. The phone continued its incessant shrill.

All he wanted was a bit of silence. A brief little shush so he could concentrate. Moreno placed the gun on the desk and looked at it. Something wasn't right.

He wasn't the type to make elaborate plans. He wouldn't leave a suicide note or funeral instructions. But Pete Moreno knew he couldn't commit suicide just yet. He didn't have the resolve for suicide yet. But there was a way he could find the resolve.

A grin curled along the corners of his mouth. He felt something like a bolt starting to give way deep in his mind, and his thoughts began to slide toward some black abyss. He figured out what was missing—he had to take out the bastard swine who put him here. His face was strained and tired, and he was physically exhausted, but he was up to the last task he wanted to accomplish in his life.

He spit out an oath. "Kill him first," he murmured. "Then kill myself."

It was the only way. He wondered if he could get away with murder; then he laughed at himself. A murderer is handicapped by having to do the deed perfectly, leaving no incriminating details. A murderer-suicide was not so encumbered.

### *RING RING RING RING RING RING RING*

And if he was dead, he wouldn't have to listen to the goddamn phones anymore.

Now maddened to desperation, Pete's thin, resolute face hardened, and his lips set in a grim line. He crossed to his study window and looked outside with almost lifeless eyes. The grounds appeared to be clear, but it really didn't matter. Reporters with cameras be damned. He put the gun in his pocket and closed the study door behind him.

# 47

It was so quiet. He couldn't believe how quiet it was. Howard Whitley looked around Kendall campaign headquarters for the last time.

Just a few hours ago, the room was filled with boisterous celebration, news cameras everywhere, and the raising and clinking of champagne glasses toasting him.

People were running up to him from all directions, wannabes scrambling for position, crowding around him, churning like a bucketful of mice, wanting to shake his hand and compliment him.

When he walked from group to group, they parted, making way for him. They showed him respect and acknowledged his importance. Howard Whitley was now a king maker.

This was going to be just the beginning.

Whitley had a deep-rooted ambition that would never be satisfied. His success only expanded his appetite for more power. He had watched it all, enjoying it all, so damned satisfied, and he privately congratulated himself on getting his candidate elected.

Until now, everything had gone so smoothly, just as he

had planned, every detail dovetailing so perfectly. Then again, he told himself, if a man like Clinton Kendall couldn't get elected in the blue state of New Jersey, where Democrats outnumbered Republicans five to one, then he should get out of the campaign business out of sheer embarrassment.

Kendall had given a brilliant victory speech. He followed Whitley's suggestions perfectly. Just the right mixture of humility for being chosen to represent the people of New Jersey, sincere praise for his opponent, and a passionate call for unity now after the bitter political squabbling to solve the problems the state was facing.

Then the crowd took the celebration to The Manor. The sound of partying originating within the headquarters grew softer, then diminished until it mixed into the distant noises from the street.

Whitley stayed behind to gather some paperwork and spend some time alone, planning a strategy for the senator-elect. It played out in his memory like the last reel of a movie.

The room was completely silent now. The lights were off, and the space was filled with shadows. It was his finest night, and it was so perfect he felt like he had achieved some little fraction of immortality.

He sighed and got past the irony of that. Would he do it all over again? Well, the question was moot now, wasn't it?

He had played old-school hard politics, balls-to-the-wall stuff, a few dirty tricks here and there along the way, but he had to—this was New Jersey, after all. He learned very early that all of life was a contest where only the best players won.

Ever since man had lived in villages, the prizes went to the fastest and strongest. It was an impractical waste of time to have a stubborn moral conscience. So Whitley moved like a shark through the water, ferociously devouring the weaker and the slower.

Now that he had time for reflection, maybe he should have handled the prostitute and her journal differently. Intimidation was better than killing, but there had been no time. And he wondered about the wisdom of the smear campaign against Pete Moreno. Was it really necessary to start the whisper campaign about his private gay life? The man lost everything. Did Whitley have to strip him of everything he had?

Yes, he decided. He had responded to these issues correctly. The election was too close. Even in the true blue state of New Jersey, the occasional Republican got elected. Whitley had to make sure Kendall got the power so Whitley could control Kendall.

Now his dream of political influence dissolved faster than sugar in water.

For the most part, Howard Whitley felt no remorse, felt no fear. But now he felt agonizing pain.

He'd just been shot.

The bullet cut through and exploded within him. He looked down and saw the bullet hole in his shirt, framed by spreading blood that made the shirt stick against his skin. He'd been shot in the stomach, and the acids were poisoning him. He felt his insides turn molten like someone had ignited a furnace within him.

By the time anyone got to him, he'd be dead.

It had been after midnight when the door to the headquarters slowly opened. He had kept the door unlocked in case any party stragglers or other well-wishers wanted directions to The Manor.

Howard heard footsteps approaching slowly.

When Howard saw who it was, he laughed cruelly and scoffed. And hurled insults. At first when the killer pulled the gun, Howard couldn't believe it. It was not a gun. It was a trick of light played on the mind brought on by days of endless campaigning and too much champagne. It couldn't be a gun. But he couldn't take his eyes off it.

"You've got to be kidding. Put that thing away."

Howard Whitley took a step closer.

"Stay where you are."

Howard stopped. He saw that the hand holding the gun was trembling.

"You wouldn't shoot me. And from the way your hand is shaking, I think you'd miss even if you did pull the trigger." Howard faked a laugh, stalling for time.

His brain scoured every avenue of possible escape, every negotiation, every deal he could make with the killer to let him live. He refused to accept the ridiculous possibility that he was about to be murdered on the night of his greatest victory.

But in spite of his strong defiance, the hallucination did not go away. In front of him was the shattering truth.

"You took everything I had," the killer said.

"Look, I can help you. If there's anything you want . . ."

"There's only one thing I want now."

Whitley knew he couldn't make a deal for his life.

There was the killer with a finger crooked around the trigger. The finger inched backward.

The interesting thing was, when his murderer aimed the gun and fired, Howard had understood completely. After what he had done to his killer to ensure Kendall's victory, Howard knew he would have done the very same thing.

So Howard didn't gape in surprise, stagger backward and

slap his hands over his gunshot wound, or open his eyes wide in amazement. He simply fell down.

Howard had to admit, though, the timing of this was atrocious, but he knew Kendall would get through it. There'd be a scandal, of course, but Kendall had no knowledge that Whitley had killed two people, and no one could prove otherwise.

Howard had doubted the existence of God his whole life, and that didn't change now in these final moments. Maybe that's why it had been so easy for him to take the lives of two people.

He had no interest in being a good person or a bad person. He only believed in figuring out how to obtain power and getting the job done to seize it. He never thought of himself as a murderer, but he always knew he was capable of it. Hell, he had actually had fun killing the people who got in his way.

No pearly gates for him, no choirs of angels, and he didn't regret that.

He momentarily regretted, though, that he was not close to his family and that he had never found the right homogeneous political wife to suit him, someone who could give him two or three homogeneous children, a family that could have furthered his own ambitions, but he quickly gave up on that thought.

He never had time for relationships, and sex was only a bedroom routine, performed without any particular love. He never trusted the idea of love. You gave over to someone else the power to wound and betray. So he had kept his distance.

He was never the type to dwell on what might have been. He accepted that there weren't many who would mourn his death. Time was up on his fifteen minutes of fame.

Oh, well, he thought, life sucks and then you die.

Suddenly the whole world seemed to have been bleached white. Howard took his last breath, succumbed to extinction, and let the whiteness envelop him.

Later, police would comment privately that Howard Whitley died looking straight ahead, coldly and calculating, as if ready and confident to confront whatever was coming next.

# 48

"You know what I like best about being a private detective?"

"What?"

"There's no paperwork. I go in, solve the case, and go home. Let the police go talk to and arrest Howard Whitley."

"You know what I like best about you being a private detective?"

"What?"

"You don't have to carry a gun, and your chances of getting hurt are reduced considerably."

"That's true. Except for hurting my hand on Brandeal's face, I think the worst thing that's happened to me since I quit the job is a paper cut."

Slick put away her notes on the Roxley/Marchinko murders. She hoped she had done right by Gloria. The dreams had stopped. She was ready to get away. "Another case solved. The fun part is over," she said.

"Now we can get started on our fun," Laura said. "Are you packed?"

"Almost done. I started packing weeks ago. I've been

looking forward to getting you alone on a cruise ship, then on a private beach. Are we going on Rosie and Kelli's ship?"

"No, not this time. We're going on Olivia Cruises. No family or kids. Besides, Rosie is busy working on her next project."

"What's that?"

"It's a game show she and Donald Trump are working on together called *Can't We All Just Get Along*. It features two teams where everyone hurls insults at each other."

"Sounds promising. Is this the Olivia Cruise where Melissa gives her Up Close concerts?"

"That's the one. Plus the Indigo Girls will be there and Kate Clinton, and I think Cherry Jones will have a night of her selected short-story readings. You know, like she does on NPR."

"Thank you, Olivia Cruises," Slick said gratefully. "Two whole weeks in the Caribbean, sipping rum drinks with little paper umbrellas stuck in pieces of fruit. Away from everything, just the two of us."

"Just the three of us." Laura looked over to Garbo, wearing a sailor hat and sitting on a little doggie suitcase.

"Of course. Just the three of us. What did we do before pet-friendly vacations?"

"We'd have to put Garbo in the ken—"

Garbo's ears shot up.

"Don't even mention the K word," Slick warned.

"I can't wait to sleep in late in the mornings, ushering in one gorgeous day after another of blank lazy inertia. I hope it will be my most unproductive weeks, ever," Laura said.

Slick pictured long starry nights on the ship with moonlight reflecting off the wine-dark water and filling their cabin, and Laura breathing softly beside her, her lips parted just a bit and her golden hair spread over the pillow.

Sometimes she would roll over, and Slick would feel Laura's breasts against her own, leading to a little night magic.

Hours later, a big butter-colored sun would be shining, streaming in their cabin balcony and waking them in the afternoon.

Sweet, Slick thought.

"I can't wait to see you by the pool in that itsy-bitsy teeny-weeny bikini." Slick looked at Laura as she moved around the room, trying to envision it. Laura was irresistible. Whatever she was saying or whatever she was wearing, she was captivating. The very scent of this woman was alluring.

Slick realized she must be insane. This woman was going to be in the middle of the ocean in a bikini with a boatload of lesbians.

And, like goldfish, lesbians have been known to eat their own.

"Ya know what," Slick said in a moment of insecurity, "let's just stay home. We don't need beaches, just a bathtub filled with bubbles, champagne, and us."

"People are expecting us," Laura said. "We've had this planned for months. Friends shuffled vacation time around so we could go as a group."

"Will we snorkel?" Slick asked. There was mischief in her eyes.

"You're making me blush."

"We can find a secluded cove and surrender to the sand and sea, nothing on our bodies but tanning lotion."

"You can be my catch of the day."

"I will be your catch of every day. Laura, do you still have that mermaid costume?"

"Yes."

"Excellent! Bring it."

"Do you still have that SpongeBob SquarePants costume?"

"Yes."

"Excellent! Bring it."

Slick hurried off happily to her closet to get the costume.
Laura watched her go and chuckled to herself. Even with her
Halle Berry good looks, Slick looked absolutely ridiculous in
the costume, and when people saw her in it, they thought she
was a nerd.

This was confirmed by the looks of sympathy she received
when Slick wasn't watching. Laura just shrugged and returned
their looks with the humiliated long-suffering-partner demeanor.

Laura trusted Slick completely. Slick had never looked at
another woman in all the time they'd been together, but
women were always looking at her, and Laura could see them
look. She was just taking out a little insurance. After all, they
were going to be sailing on a boat full of women.

Slick emerged from her closet with the SpongeBob Costume.

"Do you want me to slip it on now?" Slick asked seductively.

"No, no. It's hard to resist, but let's save some enchantment for the ship."

Slick vamped around the room, holding the costume
close, winking flirtatiously, giving Laura a coming attraction
of what to expect.

Laura smiled at her coyly. "Won't the girls envy me?"

"I can't believe I forgot to pack it."

"Oh, I wouldn't have let you forget it," Laura assured her.

"Thanks for reminding me. I'll be the life of the party
in this."

And that party will be over by 8:00 P.M., Laura thought.

"You sure will, baby," Laura lied. "I'll be especially happy to see you wear it," she added as an atonement.

Slick smiled in anticipation and put the costume into her suitcase.

"Okay, then," she said, rubbing her hands together. "Let the gay-cation begin. Where's the checklist?"

"Right here," Laura said, and handed her a notepad.

"Let's go. Tickets?"

"Check."

"Passports?"

"Check."

"Matching *Dames at Sea* sweatshirts?"

"Check. All three of them," Laura said, pointing to the little Yorkie-size shirt.

"Very good! Now, did you remember the essentials?"

"Of course. Books from the *New York Times* Best Sellers list, which we'll pretend to read, and the trashy gay novels that we really will read."

Slick laughed.

"What's so funny?" Laura asked.

"I can just see Judson down at the Pulp Friction bookstore, looking in the racks for the latest lesbian books."

"I'm sure he called and had them delivered."

"I'm sure, too, but it's a great image, isn't it?" Slick cleared her throat, stood stiffly, and went into her best Judson-the-very-proper-English-butler impersonation. "Pardon me, miss. Do you have *The Vagina Burbles at Midnight* by Portia DuQueef and *Going Down in Flames* by Calienta Hymenez?"

"Yes, we do," Laura said, playing along.

"And I'd also like the latest who-done-it."

"*The Killings Were Ax-idental?*"

"No, no, the other one. The one about the insane lesbian hatchet murderess."

"Oh, that would be *The Beaver Cleaver.*"

"Splendid! Yes, that's the one."

They both began to laugh out loud.

There was a knock on their bedroom door. Laura opened it, and there stood Judson, eyes focused straight ahead, heels together, and arms tightly against his sides.

"Judson! We were just talking about you. Come in, won't you?"

"Thank you, miss."

He entered and as always, he was formal, dignified, and solemn.

Slick and Laura tried their best to be poised. They did not want Judson to think they were joking about him behind his back. They both adored him.

"I apologize for the intrusion, miss, but there is a bit of a situation that requires your immediate attention."

"A situation?"

"Yes, miss. A Captain DeStasio wants to see you both in his office."

"Now?"

"Yes, now, miss. At once."

"Why? We just wrapped up the case."

"It seems there's been another murder, Miss Slick."

Slick and Laura exchanged a puzzled look.

"Who?" they asked in unison.

"A Mr. Howard Whitley has been found murdered at Kendall's campaign headquarters this morning."

Slick and Laura exchanged another look, then looked, crestfallen, at their luggage. The trip was going to have to be canceled.

They sighed and sagged and imagined themselves standing on the dock, waving good-bye as the Olivia cruise ship sailed out to sea without them.

Garbo, sensing what was going on, curled up on the floor, despondent. She had just had a day of beauty at the A-1 Poodle Palace in preparation for her voyage.

"Shall I cancel the reservations, miss?"

"Yes, please do, Judson."

"I shall see to it."

"Thank you."

"I've had Miss Slick's car brought 'round."

"Thanks, Judson. I'll meet you downstairs, Laura." Slick went ahead to get the car.

"Okay," Laura said after her. "I'll get our coats." Laura walked to the closet.

"Most regrettable, miss, about your vacation," Judson said as he surveyed the luggage and other vacation paraphernalia.

"Yes, it is, Judson," Laura replied, emerging from the closet. "The best laid plans . . . what?"

Laura had stopped in her tracks to look at her butler, the man who had practically helped raise her from a child.

"What did you say, Judson?"

"I said 'the best laid plans,' miss."

She looked deeply into his eyes and wondered if he was laughing at her, but his face, as usual, was inscrutable. Was he making a joke? Laura wondered. Was there a hint of amusement on his thin lips? She really couldn't tell. Laura just smiled at him with uncertainty and walked away, remembering that *The Best Laid Plans* was the title from one of the trashy gay novels they had taken on their last vacation.

When he was sure Laura had gone, Judson allowed himself a wee bit of a chuckle.

## This Is Action News 10 in New Jersey . . . All of New Jersey All of the Time

**Breaking News!!**

"Good morning. It's seventeen minutes after the hour. I'm Michelle Tevotino with a breaking news story. News 10 in New Jersey has just learned that Howard Whitley, campaign manager for Senator-elect Clinton Kendall, has been found murdered inside the senator's campaign headquarters in West Orange.

"We go live to our reporter on the scene, Scott Thompson, who has been following the story for us all morning. Scott, what do we know so far?"

"Well, Michelle, this is a stunning development. I'm standing in front of Clinton Kendall's campaign headquarters. You can see the signs of victory and 'WE WON' everywhere, the remnants of celebration. There's a huge placard that says 'Thank you, voters of New Jersey,' and now, tragically, there are flashing red and blue lights from police squad cars all around me.

"The police have a cordon of yellow tape set up; uniformed officers are examining every inch of the area, because this is now a crime scene.

"As you know, Clinton Kendall just won the Senate race in New Jersey less than six hours ago, and now his campaign manager has been found shot to death inside the senator's campaign headquarters. The police say they have no suspects in Whitley's murder, but News 10 in New Jersey has just learned that the police had wanted to question Howard Whitley in the recent killings of two former prostitutes.

"They're not saying that Whitley was a suspect in these murders; they're only saying that Whitley was a person of interest to the police."

"Have we heard anything yet from Senator Kendall?"

"Kendall is expected to hold a news conference later this morning. And that's politics in New Jersey, Michelle. Kendall was just voted into office by a landslide, and only a few hours later, he faces his first scandal, and it's a big one. I'm Scott Thompson, reporting live for News 10 in New Jersey from Kendall campaign headquarters. Back to you, Michelle."

"Thank you, Scott. Keep us posted.

"And we'll be going back to Scott throughout the day for updates as they become available.

"In entertainment news, New Jersey's own American Icon contestant Alison Sharpino has been asked to leave the show because of the pornographic pictures posted on her Web site. And Whitney Houston has been slated to join the cast of *The L-Word*. Houston will be playing the part of a closeted lesbian superstar who loses everything in a downward spiral after a fake marriage and drug addiction.

"Let's check in now with the News 10 Weather Center and give you the forecast for the weekend. And for that, let's go to meteorologist Jim St. John.

"Hi, Jim."

"Hi, Michelle. Could you ask for a more beautiful day? It looks like lots of sunshine heading our way today and a very pretty picture going forward for the weekend . . ."

# 49

Slick and Laura stormed into the police department with so much force that the double doors slammed back on their hinges.

They rushed past the chaos of crooks, hookers, and rapists being booked in the jail lobby, then went to the sergeant's desk to get visitor's passes and hurried up the three flights of stairs to the Homicide division.

As always, there were plainclothes detectives sitting at their desks taking statements, staring at computer screens, or doing paperwork.

The receptionist checked them in and waved them down the hall to Interrogation Room One. An officer stood outside to make sure no one brought a weapon inside. Slick and Laura submitted to the search. He opened the door for them, and Slick closed the door after she and Laura were inside.

Captain DeStasio was there drinking a cup of coffee and looking through a one-way window.

"Hi, Slick. Laura," he said, extending his hand to them.

"Captain," they both said in unison.

"I hope this isn't too inconvenient, but I knew you'd want to know what was going on in the case."

"What is going on?" Slick asked.

"Take a look for yourself."

She peered into the little room with the uncomfortable straight-back chairs and the harsh overhead lighting.

There was her old partner, Sam, questioning a suspect.

Though he was clearly disheveled after a long night of interrogation, Sam was grilling Pete Moreno.

"All right, let's do it again. Where were you last night?"

Pete Moreno cleared his throat. "I was home," he answered.

"Can anyone swear to that?"

"I was alone."

"Where was your wife?"

"She left me."

"Your kids?"

"She took them with her."

"So you were all alone?"

"Yes."

"How convenient. With a gun?"

"I own a gun for protection."

"If we check, we'll find you have a permit for this gun?"

"Yes, of course."

"So you went for your gun?"

"Yes."

"You were home alone. Did someone show up at your front door and threaten you?"

"No."

"So why did you suddenly need your gun?"

"I was going to kill myself."

"But you didn't?"

"Obviously not."

"So you killed Howard Whitley instead?"

"No. No. I didn't. I never wanted to hurt him."

"Well, he's dead now."

"But I didn't kill him."

"Howard Whitley ruined your life."

"I didn't blame him."

"You didn't blame the man who cost you the election and your family?"

"I didn't like him, but I wasn't going to kill him. He was too powerful."

Sam looked skeptical.

"It's politics," Moreno said. "I may have needed him in the future."

"I thought you were going to kill yourself. How would you have needed him in the future?"

"Look, I can't explain."

"You better explain."

"It's politics. Your enemy in this campaign may be your friend in the next."

"You'll forgive me if I don't take your word for it."

"You have my gun. It wasn't fired. Check the ballistics."

"Don't worry; we will."

"Good. Then you'll know I didn't shoot Howard Whitley. I didn't shoot anyone."

"But Howard Whitley is dead. Maybe you had someone kill him for you."

"I didn't."

"You admit that you left your house with a loaded gun?"

"I never left my house."

"Your gun was loaded and you were going to leave your house?"

"I was going to kill someone else."

"Who were you going to kill?"

Pete Moreno looked down and hesitated.

"Who were you going to kill?" Sam repeated, this time more forcefully.

"Jerry Jankowski."

"The male prostitute who outed you on television?"

"Yes."

"Did you kill him?"

"No, but I wanted to."

"We can't locate Jankowski."

"Look, I was upset. I lost everything, and the phone wouldn't stop ringing. It just wouldn't stop ringing. Yes, I picked up the gun. I was going to use it to kill Jerry and then commit suicide. But before I left the house, I answered the phone. It was driving me crazy. It had been ringing forever."

"So who was calling you?"

"Jim McGreevey."

"Jim McGreevey? Are you kidding?"

"Am I laughing?"

Sam glared at him intensely.

Moreno held up his hands in self-defense. "Sorry," Moreno said quickly.

Sam resumed his questioning. "The former governor of New Jersey called you?"

"Yes. He was calling to offer moral support. He told me to stay strong. Even though I was gay and had been with a male prostitute, my wife took our kids and left me, and maybe I had no future in politics, these were not reasons to give up. He convinced me my life wasn't over. I could probably get a book deal. People would want to hear my story. So you see, I never left the house. I never killed Jerry Jankowski or Howard Whit-ley. Jim McGreevey saved my life."

Slick turned to Captain DeStasio. "Has his gun been fired recently?"

"Ballistics aren't in yet. We don't know if Moreno's gun was fired or if the bullet that killed Whitley matches Moreno's gun."

"Has anyone talked to Jerry Jankowski?"

"We haven't been able to find him yet. He seems to have disappeared."

"Maybe he killed Whitley."

"Could be. Whitley was supposed to pay him big bucks to bring down Moreno. Maybe the deal went bad. Candace Moreno, Pete's wife, has a motive, too."

"I'll check her out. Can I assume that we can rule out Brandeal in this murder? That he didn't go after the man who killed Gloria Roxley?" Slick asked.

"We can rule out Brandeal," DeStasio said.

"You sound positive."

"I am. Brandeal has an airtight alibi for his whereabouts last night."

"Where was he?"

"He was at St. Alphonse's. I escorted him there myself. He's going to clean up his act."

Slick didn't need to ask any further questions about Bran-deal. It was known that St. Alphonse had a rehab program and AA meetings for cops.

# 50

Slick rolled her SLK 350 to a stop in front of the palatial home of Candace Moreno's parents. When they rang the bell, Candace herself answered.

She stood tall and reserved, wrapped in a blue-lined designer dress. She reached out and gave them both a cool, firm, bony handshake as she showed Slick and Laura to the living room.

They walked through a high narrow hallway into a wide and airy space that flowed through sliding glass doors onto a patio of dazzling tile. The pool outside sparkled in the late afternoon sun.

She indicated for them to sit down.

As soon as they sat, an olive-skinned man appeared from the hallway carrying a silver tray. Mrs. Moreno nodded, and the man put the tray down on the table between Slick and Laura and Mrs. Moreno.

On the tray were three china cups, a silver coffeepot, and matching silver creamer and sugar bowl. The whole thing jangled softly as the tray hit the table. The tray looked heavy, and the servant seemed relieved to be rid of it.

"That will be all," Mrs. Moreno said.

He bowed silently and left.

Without asking, Mrs. Moreno poured the coffee, passed Slick and Laura each a cup, then offered them cream and sugar. It was all so flawless, Laura thought, that she must have spent years perfecting it. Mrs. Moreno poured a cup for herself and seemed to settle into the situation. Slick and Laura waited for her to take a sip, then put her cup down before speaking.

"Thank you for seeing us, Mrs. Moreno," Slick said. "We know this is a difficult time."

"Yes, it is. My family warned me about politicians. Perhaps I should have listened to them."

Slick and Laura didn't know if this was a joke or not, so neither responded. They waited for her to speak again.

"How can I help you?"

Her mouth moved very little. She had a way of pressing her lips together that also hemmed the corners of her eyes, as if to keep out the light. Her voice was clear and clipped without any identifiable accent.

"Howard Whitley was found murdered," Slick said.

"Yes, I've heard the news."

"We need to ask you some questions."

"Of course. I was expecting a visit from the police."

"Do you own a gun?"

"No. My husband does, but I don't."

"Do your parents?"

"I've just moved back in with them. They never did while I was growing up. I'd be very surprised if they did now."

"Where were you last night?"

"Here."

"All night?"

"Yes. I haven't felt much like socializing lately." Then Mrs.

Moreno started to laugh. "Oh, I understand now. You think I may have had something to do with Howard Whitley's death. I thought you were merely checking up on where my husband was."

"Your husband is being questioned also," Slick said.

"Well, I certainly didn't kill him."

"We're talking to everyone who may have had a motive."

Mrs. Moreno looked at Slick severely. "My husband was dragged kicking and screaming out of the closet by Howard Whitley. But Howard Whitley was not responsible for my husband's disgusting activity. I had no motive to kill Howard Whitley."

"By disgusting activity, do you mean that he was gay?"

"No, I mean that he went to prostitutes. He betrayed me with prostitutes."

"You had absolutely no idea that he was gay?"

"Not a clue. His life was a meticulously maintained lie. I believe that if he had never been found out, he would have carried this secret to his grave."

"Maybe it was just easier to keep your suspicions to yourself."

"What do you mean?"

"Being the wife of a rich and powerful man has its perks."

"I don't deny that. But that wasn't the reason I married him. I loved him. I thought he loved me. I don't know if being gay is a choice. But marriage is definitely a choice. And he made that choice. And what about me? Do I blame my husband for being what he is, or do I blame society and my church for enabling a sham marriage that has little chance of survival?"

Slick didn't know what to say, but she felt some unexpected sympathy for Mrs. Moreno.

"Is there anyone who can verify your whereabouts last night?"

"My parents and my children."

"We may be contacting them later."

"Certainly."

As Slick and Laura turned to leave, Mrs. Moreno had one last comment. She was cold but still well mannered. "Detective, I recognize Ms. Charles here. We travel in the same social circles. I believe you said something earlier about the perks of being involved with the rich and powerful? That's a very nice Mercedes you've got. Did your work as a detective pay for that?"

Slick felt her neck burning as if hot coals had been laid across it. She knew her face was red.

"Thank you again for seeing us," Laura interjected. "We'll be in touch if we have any additional questions."

Slick and Mrs. Moreno exchanged polite good-byes.

# 51

The servers brought out the Wellfleet oysters on the half shell with champagne granité and smoked steelhead caviar, and a bottle of expensive Viognier.

They poured a taste for Slick's approval. She sipped it and nodded.

While one server poured, the other lit the candle on the table and announced the dinner for the evening. "Tonight's selection is Moscato-grilled quail stuffed with black granola, figs, prosciutto, apples, and rose petals."

"Thank you," Laura said.

"Chef said to remind you to save room for dessert, miss."

"What is it tonight?" Laura asked.

"Chocolate parfait with roasted peanut bisquit, caramel, chocolate creameux, and peanut-brittle ice cream."

"Wonderful," Laura said.

The servers bowed and left.

Slick and Laura toasted each other's stemmed wineglasses.

Slick looked at the oysters and caviar in front of her, then glanced around the huge room with the fireplace and the crystal chandelier. "Do you ever think I'm with you for your money?"

"Never."

"Not even at first?"

"Not even then."

"Why? Did you do a background check on me?" Slick said, only half kidding.

"No, of course not." Laura laughed.

"If I had as much money as you, I'd be checking people out regularly."

"No, you wouldn't; you're not that cynical."

"Maybe not, but I'm not as trusting as you are, either."

"Slick, I know when people cozy up to me for my money. My father was shrewd. He taught me to be shrewd. You've never asked me for a dime. You've never taken money you didn't earn."

"That's just it. I am now. I share your money. I didn't earn it."

"Well, if you want to get technical, then I didn't earn it, either; most of it was left to me."

"But still . . ."

"I want to share with you. I love you. My parents are gone. I don't have any brothers or sisters. If I had fallen in love with someone else, I'd be sharing what I have with them. But, poor you, I fell in love with you."

Slick was thoughtfully turning the wineglass with her fingertips.

"Sometimes I wonder if I'm getting too comfortable with it, like I'm taking advantage."

"I want you to be comfortable. I know when I'm being taken advantage of, and that's not your style."

"Look at this meal. I would never be able to afford this."

"We don't eat like this every night."

"Often enough."

"It's not half bad, is it?"

"It's delicious. It's just that sometimes I am very aware of how rich you really are, and I would never live like this without you."

"We haven't had this discussion in a long time. Mrs. Moreno really got to you, didn't she?" Laura reached across the table and squeezed her hand.

"Yes."

"Wouldn't you love me if I didn't have the money?"

"Of course."

"And I'd love you even if you had Bill Gates's money."

Slick laughed. "Fat chance! I couldn't even imagine that. I am poor. My family is poor."

"Now maybe you understand. I've always had money. It's part of who I am. I can't be separated from that any more than you can be separated from who you are."

Slick was silent for a time, then said, "Well, if one of us has to be rich, I'm glad it's you." She raised the wine and took a sip.

"I'm glad it's me, too," Laura teased.

Slick almost spit out the wine, then recovered her voice. "Spoken like a rich Republican," she said.

"Shut up and eat, you idiot. We have a case to solve."

"Okay," Slick said, picking up the little oyster fork, "but tomorrow we're going to The Olive Garden. My treat."

Slick's cell phone rang. Normally she wouldn't have answered during dinner, but she recognized Sam's work number. "I need to take this call, Laura. It's from Sam. Excuse me."

"Take it here. If it's about the case, I want to know what's going on."

Slick took the call while Laura poured them both more wine.

"Hey, Sam, what's up?" Slick listened closely. When she ended the call, she took a sip of the wine.

"So what's going on?" Laura asked.

"Jerry Jankowski went voluntarily into the police station to give a statement. No one could find him, because he was on his way to Miami, Florida, to the Lacy Centre for Sexual Reassignment. That's what he needed the fifty thousand dollars for."

"He came back on his own?"

"Yes, he felt so bad about what he did to Moreno; he didn't want to be a missing person with it hanging over Moreno's head that he may have been murdered."

"So you've crossed Jankowski off the list of suspects in Whitley's death?"

"Yes, he was traveling at the time."

"Okay, then there's Kendall, Moreno, Mrs. Moreno . . ."

Slick was silent and thoughtful. "There's only one person with nothing left to lose by killing Howard Whitley."

# 52

Mrs. Roxley sat in her rocker, her thin fingers laced together. She was staring at her cat without seeing it, concentrating on her story. All she could see was Howard Whitley as clearly as if he was in the room looking back at her.

"Can I get you something to drink? Some water, or tea, or something?" Slick asked.

"No, thank you, I'm fine." Her eyes never moved; they continued to stare ahead.

"You know that Howard Whitley was murdered and that the police are still looking for the killer?"

"Yes, I know."

"It was you, wasn't it? You killed him."

"Yes, I did," she answered truthfully. "When I saw my baby lying in the morgue, I made a promise to her."

"Tell me what happened."

Mrs. Roxley closed her eyes, bowed her head, and took a deep breath as if gathering strength from some inner spiritual place. Slick waited patiently for her to speak.

"I went to see him. I just wanted to ask him why. He barely looked at me. 'I'm busy,' he said. I asked him, 'Do you

know who I am? Do you know what you've done to me?'
He looked at me with cold eyes and said, 'Do you know who
I am? Do you have any idea how I can hurt you?' He didn't
touch me, didn't lay a hand on me, but his words were as real
as fingers around my throat.

"I brought the gun with me only for my own protection.
I knew Howard Whitley killed my Gloria. He was a dangerous man, but I had no intention of killing him."

The image of what Whitley had done to TJ Marchinko
flashed through Slick's mind. "He was a very dangerous man,"
Slick said softly. "He killed TJ. You know, Tommy, Gloria's
friend, and I think he killed Gloria, too."

"I know he did. He laughed at me. Was that other man
involved? That Clinton Kendall?"

"No, ma'am, I don't think so. I think Whitley wanted
Gloria's diary so he could always have something on Kendall,
plus there was a lot of information in there about other men
who Howard Whitley could have blackmailed to further his
power and influence."

"I'm glad about that. I voted for Kendall."

Slick couldn't stop the smile that came to her lips. "Where
did you get the gun?" she asked.

"From Gloria. She gave it to me for protection before she
left. She wanted to take me with her, but this is my house. I'm
too old to leave it, plus I'm sick. I didn't want to be a burden
to her."

"What happened next with Whitley?"

"I reached into my purse. My fingers groped for it. Drew
it out. After I found the gun, I just stood there balancing it in
my hand. I knew I had to kill him or he would kill me. It was
in his eyes. They became ugly and dangerous. Lord, how my
hands trembled."

"Where is the gun now?"

"It's in my room. I'll get it for you."

She dragged herself out of the rocker and went into her bedroom. When she returned, she laid the gun that she used to kill Howard Whitley on the table where she served her guests tea and coffee and store-bought cookies.

Both Slick and Mrs. Roxley looked down at it almost in disbelief.

Mrs. Roxley broke the silence. "Whitley took away my daughter's chance at a new beginning, a new life, so I took his. I know it was wrong, but I'm not sorry about that. I'll meet him in the next life and be judged there."

Slick picked up the gun carefully and put it in a plastic bag.

Mrs. Roxley returned to her rocking chair. "The police are going to find other fingerprints on the gun, Cassie," she said as she sat down.

"Other than yours and Gloria's?" Slick asked, surprised.

"Yes."

"Who else has handled the gun?"

"Do you know Lady Dijionnaise and Sheleeta Buffet?"

"Yes, ma'am, I do," Slick said, shaking her head and wondering what they did now.

"They have been like family to me since Gloria died. They check on me. Make sure I get my medicine. Whatever I need. All I have to do is pick up the phone. Someone from Halsey Street comes by to see me every day. I put Lady and Sheleeta in charge of my final arrangements. I told them I killed Howard Whitley, so they had a lot of their friends from Halsey Street come over and handle the gun. They don't want me to be bothered in my last days, and selfishly I agree with that. Lady said their friends have so many police records, it would take the police years to figure out who killed Whitley."

"Lady is right about that," Slick said, smiling.

"Do you have to tell the police about that right away?"

"I'll only tell Captain DeStasio."

"Fair enough. Lady and Sheleeta tell me he's a good man."

"May I ask why were you so sure it was Whitley who killed Gloria?"

Mrs. Roxley said nothing.

"It was Brandeal, wasn't it? He must have called or come by after we all met in DeStasio's office."

"You make it sound like a tip-off. It was more like a concerned man calling a dying woman to let her know the man responsible for her daughter's death would be brought to justice. He didn't know I'd do what I did. I couldn't wait for court justice. I can't go to my little girl knowing the man responsible for her death was still walking around."

"I've known Brandeal for a long time. He's garbage. Why would he care about you or Gloria?"

Mrs. Roxley looked at her with disapproval. "Now, Cassie, you know I don't let garbage in my house. Mr. Brandeal had been trying to get Gloria off the street for a long time. That's why Gloria felt so comfortable turning to him for help. And Gloria told me that was the reason he would never officially register her as an informant. He was afraid for her safety and didn't want it documented anywhere that she had been cooperating with the police. And if he had been successful in getting her off the street, he didn't want the record to surface. I'm grateful to him for all he did. So please do not refer to that man as garbage in front of me."

"Yes, ma'am. I'm sorry."

"I don't know what went on between you and Mr. Brandeal, but I'm certain he loved Gloria in his own way, but he also knew it wouldn't work out between them. That was why he had risked so much to help her disappear, and when it went wrong, it almost killed him."

Slick let this sink in for a moment. The irony of Slick and Brandeal loving the same woman was not lost on her. Was it possible that the man she had openly disdained had a streak of decency? She thought back over all the things Brandeal had done. No way. Brandeal had earned every bit of that disdain. This was one isolated episode in a career of unethical behavior. She wasn't going to change her mind about him, but neither would she start listing his sins to a dying woman who might be the only person who ever thought anything kind about him.

"I have to ask you, Mrs. Roxley—did anyone drive you to or from Kendall's headquarters?"

"No, I'm slow, but I can still take the bus. Old people are invisible. No one pays us much attention. I got there and back on my own." Mrs. Roxley reached for something hidden in the cushion behind her. "Here, Cassie, I want you to have this," she said as she handed Slick an envelope. "I've written it all down. My confession. I guess I'm giving you my own diary."

Slick was suddenly overwhelmed with sadness. She knew she had only a few conversations left with Mrs. Roxley.

"Cassandra, don't you feel bad. Look at me, Cassandra. Look at me. I've lived a long time, a lot of it good. Ain't no tragedy in an old woman dyin'."

Then Mrs. Roxley smiled. She was calm and placid. She drifted away from Slick as if seeing and hearing something Slick could not.

# 53

"Captain?"

"Hey, Slick. Thanks for stopping by. Have a seat."

Slick sat in the same chair as always when in DeStasio's office.

DeStasio studied her face before he spoke. He was uncertain of how to tell her. Then he leaned back and spoke softly. "I'm putting in my papers. I got the time."

Slick wasn't prepared for this. She thought DeStasio would be there until he was dragged out.

"You're kidding!"

"No, I'm serious."

"Why?"

"It's time. The job came to mean too much after my wife died. Funny how you don't know you're relying on someone for their strength. You think it's your own. My wife, this job. Those were the only things I had that defined me. Plus, I lost my perspective on this case with Brandeal. And that's something you can't afford to lose."

Slick had had many conversations over the years with DeStasio, but this was the first time she had the opportunity

to tell him what she thought of him. "You've done good police work here, Captain. This district had a drop in crime
when you took over, and it's still down. People can walk the
streets at night without fear. Parents can send their children to
the corner store knowing that they will get there and back
safely."

"Thank you, Slick, but I'm too old for this. It's better for
all of us if I go. I need something more." DeStasio let his eyes
sweep over his office. God, he was tired. "Anyway, I'm done.
My last day is next Friday."

"It's none of my business, but what will happen to Paula?"

"What do you mean?"

"She solicited false statements from Lady and Sheleeta."

"Did she? It turns out that Brandeal really did grab Paradise off the street. I see no reason to pursue that."

"And Mrs. Roxley's gun and confession?"

"Sam's in charge of the case. I gave him the necessary
info. I'm sure he'll handle it properly."

Slick nodded her understanding. "You know what you're
going to do after you retire?"

"What do you think I'm going to do? I'm going to move
to Florida and fish."

"You know how to fish?"

"I can learn."

They shared a small laugh.

"I want to leave without a lot of hoopla. I can't avoid
everything, though. I guess there'll be an office party. I'll get a
gold watch or something. It would mean a lot to me if you
were there."

"Of course I'll be there. Laura and I will both be there."

DeStasio gave her a grateful smile.

She stood up and walked to his desk, then reached into

her pocket and pulled out her little tin badge and threw it on his desk.

He looked at it and smiled. "I can't believe you still have that thing."

"I kept it."

"That was a lot of years ago."

"When I was a kid, whenever I was about to do something stupid, I looked at this badge and remembered the police officer who took the time to come to my door, give this to me, and salute me. It kept me on the straight and narrow. You're the reason I became a police officer."

"You solved a murder and you weren't even out of grade school. No way you couldn't become a cop."

They took the moment and laughed together, remembering.

Slick spoke softly. "My parents were grateful to you. They really weren't sure what was going to happen to me."

"How is your mom?"

"She misses my dad, but she's hanging in there."

"Give her my best."

"Will do."

Slick put the badge back in her pocket, then shook DeStasio's hand.

"Good luck, sir. It's been an honor to serve with you."

Then she stood at attention and saluted Frank DeStasio, her captain, for the last time.

# Epilogue

*Six months later*

"In sure and certain hope of the resurrection unto eternal life through our Lord Jesus Christ, we commend unto our Lord, Bernice Eleanor Roxley, and we commit her body to the ground. Earth to earth, ashes to ashes, dust to dust. May the Lord bless and keep her and make His face to shine upon her and give her peace. Amen."

"Amen," the mourners replied.

Slick let her eyes roam over the cemetery. The day was beautiful. The trees were in full bloom, filled with birds singing at their loveliest. A fitting setting, she thought. When Laura squeezed her hand and smiled, Slick could tell she was thinking the same thing.

Most of the Halsey Street regulars were there to say good-bye. Slick wasn't positive, but she thought Sheleeta was holding Mrs. Roxley's cat in her lap.

Reverend Walker refocused her thoughts. "How will Bernice Roxley be remembered?" he asked. "As a loving wife,

mother, and friend. There is a creator beyond our understanding with mercy beyond our comprehension."

When the service was over, one by one, the attendees
came forward and placed a rose on the casket. In the distance,
Captain Frank DeStasio stood alone, watching.

Later, after all the mourners had left, the very last rose
placed on the casket of Bernice Roxley was from Tom Brandeal.